William James Stillman

Francesco Crispi

Insurgent, Exile, Revolutionist and Statesman

William James Stillman

Francesco Crispi
Insurgent, Exile, Revolutionist and Statesman

ISBN/EAN: 9783743310568

Manufactured in Europe, USA, Canada, Australia, Japa

Cover: Foto ©Raphael Reischuk / pixelio.de

Manufactured and distributed by brebook publishing software
(www.brebook.com)

William James Stillman

Francesco Crispi

Frontispiece.

F. CRISPI, 1863

FRANCESCO CRISPI

Insurgent, Exile, Revolutionist
and Statesman

BY

W. J. STILLMAN, L.H.D. (CONCORDIA)

LATE CORRESPONDENT TO THE 'TIMES' IN ROME;
AUTHOR OF 'THE UNION OF ITALY'; 'THE CRETAN INSURRECTION OF 1866';
'HERZEGOVINA AND THE LATE UPRISING (1878)'; 'THE OLD
ROME AND THE NEW,' ETC., ETC.

London
GRANT RICHARDS
BOSTON, U.S.A., HOUGHTON, MIFFLIN & CO.
1899

Printed by R. & R. CLARK, LIMITED, *Edinburgh.*

INTRODUCTION

FRANCESCO CRISPI: A CHARACTER STUDY

THE day after Crispi had, on the death of Depretis, assumed the presidency of the Council with the portfolio of Foreign Affairs, I found myself climbing the slope which leads to the Consulta, the palace of Foreign Affairs, in company with the Editor of the X——, one of the Roman journals of the Left, a journalist whom I had known for years, and who was one of my colleagues in the Montenegrin campaigns. He was full of faith in Crispi and his own paper as the official organ of the new order of things. " I will guarantee that in six weeks the X—— will be the official organ," said the Editor, my friend. He had his audience—a short one—and then came my turn. What I had to say, beside the formal congratulation over the accession, was that my chief had ordered me to learn the Mediterranean policy of the new ministry in order that we might support it. I delivered my message, and waited. Crispi made no

B

reply for a moment, but looked at me with a severe, repelling half-frown, did not ask me to sit down, and when, after the lapse of several minutes, the silence was not broken, I begged him to believe that I had not come from journalistic curiosity, but in pursuance of orders from the Editor in order that the paper might give his policy its support. Always looking me in the eyes with the expression of a suspicious watch-dog, he finally replied curtly, "The Government has no need of the support (*appoggio*) of the Press." "In that case, Excellency," I replied, "I have the honour to say good morning," and, turning on my heel, I walked out with my back to him, and not saluting.

The next week the *X*—— came out in the most savage opposition, and for six weeks I abstained from all intercourse with the Consulta, notwithstanding that I had among the officials of the ministry some of my best friends, ignoring it as completely as if it did not exist. At the end of that time there was in *The Times* a telegram from Suakim, telling of a collision between some Italian and English officers, and a difficulty about a question of delimitation. I then received a message from the Consulta, to request me to call on the Minister, with the assurance that "I should not make antechamber." Crispi had found that his independence of the Press was not so absolute as he supposed, and he treated me with consideration, and, having charged me with assurances of the disposition of the Government to remove any cause of difficulty on the frontiers, he did all that his always brusque manner permitted to remove the impression of our former interview.

From that time I was always received with courtesy, but not with the least invitation to intimacy, nor was it till long after, on the occasion of the Naples convention for the delimitation of the Kassala frontiers (which I attended) towards the end of his first ministry, that he became satisfied that I was a friend of Italy, by the efforts I made to remove misunderstandings that occurred in the settlement of certain questions through the mischievous misrepresentations regarding Sir Evelyn Baring (Lord Cromer) on the part of the Italian commissioners, who had persuaded Crispi that Baring was hostile to any arrangement with Italy. This falsehood did not come to my knowledge till after the breaking off of the negotiations, so that, though I had been able to remove some minor difficulties, the worst was not removed, and Sir Evelyn left for Cairo, leaving Crispi persuaded that he had to do with an enemy of Italy, with whom every inch of advantage was to be fought for. It was in the course of these negotiations that Crispi became convinced that I was a real friend of Italy, and from that time forward he was accustomed to communicate to me confidentially such matters as were of public interest for publication ; but there was, neither then nor later, the intimacy between us which English and French journals supposed, and on the strength of which supposition all my views of Italian politics were believed to be the reflection of those of Crispi. The fact was, that there was never any other intimacy between us than that of an honest minister towards an honest journalist, for Crispi is not a man to make an intimate amongst journalists, for whom in general he had a strong aversion, which was natural under the circumstances, for, except *La Riforma*, there was not a paper in Italy, so far as I know, which did not oppose him. With regard to *The Times*, he had had reason for discontent, as my predecessor had been distinctly obsequious to the Vatican, and had compromised the tone of the paper. He came to regard me as a loyal friend of Italy, and treated me as such, but beyond that there was on neither side a desire for intimate personal relations. His domestic surroundings were to me unapproachable, and I have never broken bread under his roof ; and often when affairs were uneventful I did not see him for weeks. I supported him for his English policy.

During his first administration his attitude towards the Press was one of persistent antagonism, or worse. He paid the expenses of *La Riforma*, the only journal which supported him, but, so far as I could learn, he subsidised no other, and to the foreign Press—French, German, or English—he was either contemptuous or indifferent, even to rudely refusing interviews. So far as *The Times* was concerned, after our first brush he was respectful, but never made the slightest advance towards a private understanding as to my tone in my correspondence, or hinted, either personally or through another, at any favour to be granted on account of it, nor did he ever attempt to influence me in what I should write, further than by giving me authentic information which he did not give to other correspondents, which was natural, considering the importance of *The Times*. From my first interview to my resignation in 1898 I never heard from him, or any friend or subordinate, a word, or saw an indication which indicated a desire to influence me. After he became, during the convention of Naples, convinced that I was really a friend of Italy, he gave me the Cross of the Crown of Italy, more as an admission, I supposed, of his having misjudged me in the past than from any other motive, but neither to him nor me had this a serious value, for distinctions of that kind are empty honours to him as to me. I made no overture for it, and could not in courtesy refuse it—I was, in fact, indifferent to it, and it was only given just before he fell.

The critics of my *Union of Italy* have charged me with abasing the great figure of Cavour in comparison with Crispi. The reader will see in the following pages what I think of the affairs in which they came in contact, but a comparison between them is impossible. Cavour was a parliamentary statesman, perhaps the ablest of his day in Europe, but he believed in parliaments and diplomacy alone, this side the *ultima ratio* of nations, and abhorred insurrections and the revolutionary element. Crispi was a revolutionary statesman, born and bred to conspiracies, and as such the greatest Italy has produced in our times, and, after Cavour, Crispi has the greatest intellectual political ability amongst the makers of Italy, who are—Cavour, Vittorio Emanuele, Garibaldi, Mazzini, Ricasoli, Farini, and Crispi. Cavour had always with him wind and tide, King, Court, wealth, nobility, in short, every element in the state which could strengthen his position. Crispi had poverty, exile, imprisonment, and the hostility of King, Court, and every conservative interest; and while Cavour, with the aid of all the forces of the kingdom, brought under the flag of Savoy—Tuscany by the aid of Ricasoli, Lombardy by the gift of France, the central provinces by the aid of Farini and his associates, paying for them with Savoy and Nice, Crispi and Garibaldi brought the larger half of Italy, scarcely aided except by the private patriotism of all Northern Italy. I will not anticipate what has to be said later in these pages on the regrettable conflict between men who loved Italy with equal, if different, devotion. No comparison, but contrast, is to be drawn between Cavour and Crispi. Cavour towered over everybody with whom he worked, and absorbed the individuality of all. Garibaldi and Crispi, in the expedition of the Thousand, were like Castor and Pollux ; where one was wanting the other was competent, equally patriotic, equally disinterested, and equally ready to efface themselves before each other and Italy. With all his disadvantages, Crispi stands next to Cavour in the history of the making of Italy. What he might have done or been with the favour of King, Court, and the support which Cavour had on all sides can only be conjectured.

But, owing to this antagonism and the prejudice which has grown out of it, Crispi has been misunderstood and misrepresented as no Italian, or even European, statesman has ever been. To a certain extent this is due to the character of the man, a conspirator by evolution if not by birth, secretive, reticent, conscious to excess of his own abilities, and contemptuous of the common ways of making

them known ; taciturn, moody, and indifferent
to the opinion of others to an extraordinary
degree, he paid no court to success and only
begged for Italy—for himself any hardship
was more grateful than dependence on those
who did not trust him.　Liberal Europe only
knew Italy for good in Piedmont, and for ill
in Naples, and in the early stages of revolution Crispi was conspicuous in neither.
Compelled to secrecy in all his earlier life, he
was condemned to obscurity later, because he
was considered dangerous to the ideas of men
who were able to keep him there, and who
would, had it been possible, have kept him for
ever out of public life.　Lost to the English
sight, in the crowd of conspirators and schemers ;
averse to proclamations and words, he only
emerged from the mass of the Italians of the
Regeneration when the other great luminaries
of it had gone below the horizon.　Not to be in
office is for a politician not to be known out of
one's own country, and Crispi was late in coming
to office—the reasons for which do him honour
but do not affect the fact.　Insignificant men
preceded, and followed him, partly on account
of his qualities and partly on account of the
defects of them, and when he came to the
front he was a survival of another and more
heroic epoch.　His life until 1860 was that of
a conspirator, dreaded as much by the con-
servatives who were in power, as a radical and

republican, as for his abilities, and when his convictions had brought him over to the support of royalty, and he had uttered the memorable words, " The Monarchy unites us, the Republic would divide us," and accepted the King, he was regarded by his new allies with distrust, and by his old friends with the bitterest animosity or indignation, as a deserter from the principles of the Republic.

But it is largely due to his irrepressible individuality, which revolts against being compressed into the mould of a party, or into irresponsible subordination in politics, that he has always stood alone, and much of the animosity with which he appears always to have been regarded by many of his contemporaries seems to have been due to this tendency, and to the fact that he never gives his confidence entirely to any man. His sense of personal dignity is morbidly acute, and he savagely repels any question which seems to impeach his sincerity in politics or the honourableness of his motives. His dearest friend would hardly dare to ask him for an explanation which implied a reproach to his honour or public integrity, certain to receive at best a contemptuous denial. I remember him saying once in the Chamber, in reference to some such imputation, " I do not discuss any question assailing my honour. Let my life answer for that."

He is at once the best loved and the most

hated of Italian statesmen, and the unquestionable superiority he possessed over all the heads
of the factions at times opposing, and at times
favouring him, intensified the vicissitudes of
his political life ; at one time the dictator of
the destinies of Italy, and at another a chief
without a party, compelled to look on and see
all his work undone and his adherents divided
between the factions, and following other
leaders ; for to this does the condition of
Italian politics lead, that through default of
party discipline or organisation, the only tie
between the representatives of the people is
the possession of office.

In the regard of the great majority of the
Italian people Crispi holds a position which is
secure, that of the first of the now living
statesmen of the peninsula and the last of her
great makers ; but in the corruption of their
politics, and the want of political organisation
and education, the verdict of the election is not
decisive of the character of the legislatures
issuing from it ; fidelity of the deputy to his
pre-election professions having no place amongst
the virtues of the Italian politician, so that
nothing secures the popular approbation from
being followed by a defeat in the Chamber of
Deputies. This condition of political anarchy
is in part the fault of Crispi himself. Holding
for the last twenty years the undisputed possession of the chieftainship of the democratic

element, he has never asserted his position by attempting to organise the forces of it in attack on the antagonistic parties, but when he has met with a reverse, he has retired to his tent and waited for the moment when the country should recognise the need of him. Political parties, like armies, are most solidly organised by offensive operations, and Crispi has not been willing to lead the opposition in attack and so secure its allegiance, but with a self-assertion which too closely resembles arrogance, has, when out of office, withdrawn to nearly complete isolation and inaction. While neglecting in this way the means of organising a party for the support of his ideas of government, he was yet excessive in his individual attacks on the factions, especially on the surviving fraction of the old Right which had for so many years and with such indignities hunted him on all occasions, and which were, when the opportunity offered, united in hostility to him to the last. At times he broke out in rancorous Philippics, bitter and personal beyond the just limits of parliamentary decorum, and received the compensation in return of aggravated hostility whenever occasion offered to annoy him.

Of this war, which did equal harm to Crispi and to the healthy and greatly-needed development of constitutional life in Italy, the Right was doubtless primarily responsible.

As the first political factor of the movement which brought Naples and Sicily into the kingdom of Italy, and even preceding Garibaldi in the real shaping of the event ; as a frank and courageous adherent to the Monarchy when all his former political associations had attached him to the Republic — adherence which cost him the political support of his old friends, with few exceptions—he deserved the confidence of the Royalists to whose interests he had given unreserved support ; while, in fact, he met only with distrust, hostility, and ostracism, applied in every case in which it was possible. Excluded by official pressure from the representation of Palermo in the first Italian Parliament, he only entered the Chamber he had been the first to move in the possible formation of (that of the Kingdom of Italy, accomplished by the plebiscite of annexation of Southern Italy), by the chance of having been almost clandestinely nominated in a second electoral college unknown to the Piedmontese ministry ; and at every turn he was met by distrust and hostility equal to that shown to Mazzini himself. It would have been strange if to his fiery and vindictive Sicilian temper this shameful persecution had not left permanent effects in undying hatred of the party which was responsible for it, and which maintained it unrelentingly down to the epoch of his second ministry, and which

even at the present time shows that its rancour
has not been exhausted. But the heat of
Crispi's indignation carried him at times beyond the limits of just resentment, and added
to the partisan malevolence which he would
have done better to leave for reprobation to the
judgment of posterity, and at others led him,
from the spirit of antagonism, to the denun-
ciation of the measures he had previously
supported, finding them advocated by his
opponents. And beyond the lines of the old
party antagonisms there were cases in which
he attacked with the same bitterness those of
his own side of the Chamber from whom he
happened to differ as to the measures of the
day. This mental condition is no doubt responsible for a part of the opposition which
Crispi has always provoked, and for much of
the rest the influences of the Court are answer-
able, for Crispi was always intensely obnoxious
to the world about the throne, whether from
his ancient republicanism or a certain hostility
he always cherished against the Court influences which had been against him in the
beginning, and which he regarded with
animosity for their effect on the administration
of affairs, being, in his conception of government, unconstitutional and illegitimate. In
this he was undoubtedly right, for the influences of the Court have never been other
than disastrous to the best interests of con-

stitutional government in Italy, and they are largely responsible for the demoralisation in it, and for the reaction appearing of late towards radical republicanism.

The scandal arising out of Crispi's divorce was dexterously employed by the Court against him, and the most exaggerated accusations of immorality were drawn from it, and had no doubt a great influence on his position for the time ; but if in the single transaction which that represents, his conduct was open to reproach, the conclusion drawn by his accusers of a general immorality is absolutely without justification. Crispi never was a licentious man ; his temperament prevents it, and those who know him personally know that in the mingled fire and ice of his temperament there is little place for licentiousness. The passion of his life has been the liberty of Italy, and from the day when he buried the romance of his young life in the grave of his first wife, conspiracy and affairs of State have absorbed his energies completely, and women, or even society at large, have been merely incidental. In the scandalous general condition of sexual morality in the world he moved in, Crispi is almost a manifestation of purity and continence.

Crispi's reticence and an extreme preoccupation gave him socially the credit of a moroseness which does not exist, for his nature is of the kindliest, but he has no patience with people who come merely to talk and have no serious business with him. He does not invite confidence, and with importune visitors he may be very peremptory; but his patience is unlimited in cases of injustice done. The arts of political conciliation being little known to him, no doubt he has often lost support for the want of them; but, as he has never sought power or seemed overanxious to arrive at it, there was the less reason for the cultivation of them. He, of course, expected, and doubtless desired, to be called to the Government long before he was; but he never showed impatience, and when some one taunted him with his early unsuccess he replied, " Io mi chiamo Domani "—I call myself To-morrow. Petrucelli di Gattina says that one day he asked Crispi if he was a Mazzinian. " No ! " he replied. " A Garibaldian ? " " No more." " And what are you, then ? " " I am Crispi," was the reply.

The savage, and politically as well as morally unprincipled, campaign of scandal against Crispi of 1891-93 made entirely in the interests of France and by the least responsible group of the Italian politicians, may perhaps be considered as demanding notice by one who pretends to write an unbiassed life of the statesman, and I give it all the attention it deserves, so far as public knowledge enables me to form an opinion. It would be rash in the extreme to pronounce positively on a question of public morality in the state of that virtue which prevails in Italy, but what one may safely say is that no evidence worth serious consideration of Crispi's venality or corruptibility has ever been presented, and the *a priori* conclusion which we are entitled to draw from a life of exile and poverty, repelling all concessions of principle and refusing all offers of interested advancement, is that the man against whom, at the age of seventy, no accusation of a similar character had ever been maintained, though he held at times the revenues of a province in his hands, is most unlikely in his later years to fall before a miserable temptation to barter the honour of his country. And it needs some recognition of the honesty and morality of the men who coin such accusations, to give them weight, and grounds for this recognition exist nowhere ; for, whether in sexual or fiscal morality, the state of things in Italy throws Crispi into high relief. The intense desire in certain political quarters to remove from the field of active politics the man on whose ability and perspicacity Italy could most count at the present moment, if international difficulties were to arise, accounts fully for the campaign of slander ; but to one who has known Crispi ever since he came to power, and who has no motive to bias in judging him, the extra-

parliamentary war on Crispi which occupied
the attention, more or less, of Europe so long,
is the most unscrupulous and unwarranted
political campaign in the politics of Europe
or America, in which I have been an observer
for more than forty years. Personal impres-
sions are liable to error, but at the age which
has passed the Psalmist's limits they are worth
something, and after twelve years of study of
Crispi's political conduct I am free to say that
much more evidence than anything I have
ever heard or seen must be brought forward
to induce me to question for one moment
Crispi's honesty or the purity of his patriotism.
But, like other Italian ministers, he has often
paid for the dishonesty of his supporters.

It may not be amiss that I inform my
readers that I have received no assistance from
Signor Crispi in the compilation of the following sketch, for it hardly deserves a more serious
title. He, probably wisely, seems to have
preferred to avoid any possibility of being
considered accessory to either praise or blame
of himself, and it seems difficult to avoid the
one or the other when cognisant of one's own
biography. It would have been a great advantage to me to have had access to some of
the full and contemporary accounts of the
transactions in which the Italian statesman
has taken part, and which are recorded in
diaries which in the future will be of great

interest to the historian, but which were rigidly refused me. But the biography of Crispi must wait for younger men than I am to be rendered full justice. Hate and devotion have too much hold on his present to permit entire justice to be done him in his political lifetime. For what I have written I owe most to the series of articles in the *Revue Internationale*, by Edmond Mayor, long time private secretary to Crispi ; to a charming and important little book by the same, *M. Crispi chez. M. de Bismark ;* and to the little book of my friend Vincenzo Riccio, *I Meridionali nella Camera*, for the earlier periods, and somewhat to the life of Crispi by Narjoux ; but for the later period I depend on my own observation and knowledge of his public acts.

Vincenzo Riccio, in *I Meridionali nella Camera*, has drawn Crispi's character at his first entry into the premiership (1887) in the following words, true then, but not complete, for they fail to recognise how large a part of the traits there depicted were due to the state of acute conflict and unmeasured persecution in which he had passed the greater part of his life, and which still endured, and which now must be taken as having become a part of his character :—" Too clearly has the fact proven that the temperament of Francesco Crispi is stronger than his will. In many occasions he has allowed himself to be dragged into acts

and words neither fitting nor convenient to
one who is chief of the government in a free
state. Add a pride unmeasured and unreason-
able. It seemed pride in the opposition deputy,
and therefore a virtue. It is shown to be
arrogance, and is a vice and a danger in the
minister, since it regards a man on whom
depend the most important public interests,
and who despatches them without taking
counsel of any one, following the impulses of
his own mind." Nor was the latter part of
this entirely true even in his first ministry.
In his own department he asked no advice of
his colleagues, perhaps, but he left them the
responsibility in theirs. In the banking question and crisis he allowed his better judgment
to be overruled by his colleagues, Giolitti and
Grimaldi ; and when in the crisis of the African
question he found his colleague in the ministry
of war, General Bertole-Viale, disposed to push
operations on a scale beyond the resources of
the country, he took the colony from that
ministry and transferred it to that of Foreign
Affairs, which he himself held. In this, as in
all the questions which composed the foreign
policy of Italy, he held a wise and far-reaching
policy, which he often failed to carry out
with diplomatic tact, and which in manner
rather than in matter caused needless friction.

Of the problems which gave him most
thought I think the ecclesiastical question was

the most grave and perhaps the only really difficult one *per se*, and in respect to this he showed himself considerate to all beliefs and all sincere prejudices, conciliatory to the Papacy as far as the inviolate rights of the nation permit, but ready to face any opposition where they are menaced from within or without. In religion he is a freethinker with a profound sense of the immanent Deity, sympathetic with the Orthodox Church in which he was born and bred, but with antipathy to no other; he is respected beyond all the other statesmen of Italy by the lower clergy, especially in the southern provinces, and in the Vatican he has more and warmer friends than any other minister. In ecclesiastical crises, as in all others, he had to encounter the implacable hatred of France, no matter what regime controls that country, but in this matter his policy was one of passive resistance to any resumption of old privileges by the Church, and firm maintenance of the compact made, although he had opposed it when made. With the lower clergy and their influence in general, he was in full sympathy, for it was his profound conviction that a people without religion is doomed to decay of all national virtues, and whatever may be the depth or soundness of the Roman Catholic religion as it is held by the masses in Italy, it is the best they know, and there is little probability of its ever being changed for any other form. With the Temporal power and the immixtion of the Church in politics he was always in inflexible antagonism, and to him absolute liberty of belief was a condition *sine qua non* of healthy national existence. Of his sincere religious conviction I am profoundly and with good grounds convinced, for I have on several occasions been able to see in unguarded moments his real convictions, nor has he ever hesitated to avow his belief in a controlling Deity when there was opportuneness in the declaration. On the occasion of the raising of the statue to Giordano Bruno he refused to take part in a professedly atheistic demonstration, saying, " I am not an atheist." In the evening after the last attempt on his life, I called to congratulate him on his escape, and in the course of the conversation I remarked that it seemed almost like a providential interference that a man should fire a pistol at him so near that it would have burned his hair off if it had been pointed right (the pistol was thrust into the carriage and the assassin had his hand on the carriage door), and that he should not have been harmed. He looked up from his papers into my face and with an unaccustomed solemnity which there was no mistaking, for there is not a trace of the hypocrite in him, he said, " I believe it was providential— it was a miracle." With all his official severity and maintenance of discipline, he is one of the kindest-hearted men I ever knew, and without the least ostentation, and his charity is as large and genuine as it is secret, with that secretiveness which is one of the dominant traits of his character.   One of the superior magistrates who has had much experience, and complete knowledge of the working of the law of public security of 1893, which has been the basis of the charges of despotic severity against Crispi, assured me that he reviewed every case of condemnation under it, and where any mitigating circumstances existed, he cancelled the condemnation, although it had passed through a trial before a mixed commission, and had a hearing on appeal to a higher commission, so that no innocent man could have been punished beyond the preventive imprisonment, and many who were guilty escaped.   On the other hand, he was of Rhadamanthine severity against any revolutionary attempt ; and especially the men who attempt to mislead the masses by schemes socialistic or political, found no mercy in him.   This has been even made a subject of reproach, that he, a revolutionary of the most desperate dye, should now crush those who imitate him, but he replies, " We rebelled against tyrants and government without law, but revolution *now* is against the existence of a government in which all share and the majority governs—it is a crime."

CHAPTER I

CRISPI was born at Ribera, a little town on the southern coast of Sicily, October 4, 1819, of an Albanian family which had immigrated from Northern Albania, after the defeat of the last Christian hero of the Skipetar race, Skander Beg, whose adherents migrated to Italy in thousands after the final struggle between the Cross and the Crescent, in the latter part of the fifteenth century. The grandfather of Francesco was a priest in the Orthodox Church (commonly and incorrectly called the Greek Catholic), in which the parish priests are necessarily married men, and the Albanian was the family language down to the lifetime of the statesman. To those who know the race of Skander Beg, its intellectual force, tenacity, craftiness, and curious mixture of passionless temperament with volcanic temper ; cold, calculating, and deliberate when something has to be planned, and patient and tenacious in the carrying out of the plan ; faithful to death where faith is due ; honest as day where personal fidelity demands it, and crafty as a red Indian where an enemy is to be guarded against, the character of Crispi will be the cropping out of the typical individuality of the race. The roots of the nature were Skipetar, and the training Sicilian, with neither of which has the Italian temperament anything to do, though the southern sun and its quickening have probably their share in the result.

Crispi's education was made in the " Greek-Albanian " seminary of Palermo, and in the university of the same city, which became later the seat of his professional career. At the age of eighteen he took his degree of Doctor of Laws. The education of that day was the traditional, based on the classics, and Crispi has not at the age of eighty forgotten his Tacitus and Cicero. But the practical studies which his subsequent life made so important to his success, he made in the harder school of experience. His father's intention was that he should enter into the magistracy, which was then, as it is now, not only in Italy, but in some other countries of Europe, a separate career, the preparation for which differs from that for the bar in many details, but as his age on leaving the university was not that demanded for entering the magistracy, he was admitted to the bar for the interval. Sicily was then under the full reaction from a defeated constitutional movement, and the Divine Right of the Bourbons dictated the law and regulated justice. It was the school in which a man disposed to absolutism would be at home in the magistracy, but one who at heart was a revolutionary would only find the suggestion of revolt against the system in which he lived. The short career at the bar of Palermo was only a nominal occupation. Crispi became a journalist as journalism then was understood because it gave him opportunity for the safe expression of his sympathies with freedom. He founded a journal called the *Oreteo*, from a little river which empties into the sea not far from Palermo. Discussion of politics being forbidden in the realms of the Bourbon, *Oreteo's* laudation was limited to the ancients, or was incidentally extended to the modern Greeks, who were then the heroes of the day, the glamour of their struggle for emancipation still resting on them. The Grand Turk was the pretext for the abuse of tyrants which every good subject of any Christian power could employ freely, and excite no suspicion of liberalism. In *Oreteo*, Crispi wrote poetry, essays on literary subjects, and even went so far as to denounce tyranny in the abstract and tyrants in general, but the day of revolt and conspiracy had not yet dawned, and Platonic aspirations did not disturb authority.

Crispi's early romance, more influential on

his mature life than the world suspects, is worth telling as a part of his character. During his second year at the university he lodged with a family of the Palermitan middle class, composed of a widow, one son, and four daughters. To the second daughter, Rosina, Crispi became strongly attached, and the attachment being reciprocated, he proposed to marry her, an imprudence for a youth of eighteen which the parents on both sides opposed, and on his side with practical vigour, for his father coming to Palermo, carried him away and promptly broke off all communications between the lovers. Francesco was sent to a farmhouse which belonged to the family at Sciacca, on the sea coast not far from Ribera, and kept under a sort of domestic guard. To those who know the passionate, filial devotion of the Skipetar and kindred Greek races, it will be no surprise that this relegation to bounds was an effective interdiction to intercourse between the lovers, but during this time the cholera, which had been spreading through Europe, reached Sicily and became intense at Palermo, under the effect of the ancient prejudices as to pestilence, involving seclusion and abandonment of the infested quarters to what might happen in them. One quarter, itself infected, arms in hand, forbade access to the inhabitants of others, and the dead were hardly numbered ;

from hundreds they grew to thousands daily. At Sciacca, Crispi learned of the terrible character of the disease at Palermo, and unable to get any news of his Rosina, took the horse of his father's tenant and stole away to Palermo. He found Rosina with one of her sisters only alive, the mother and the other children having died of the cholera ; and having no means of his own, he sold the horse and devoted himself and the proceeds to the sustenance of the sisters. He was mourned as dead, and only after a lapse of many days through the chance recognition of the horse, sold to the postal service, was a clue given to his whereabouts. He was found and recalled, and consent was given to the marriage. Rosina died two years later, leaving a young daughter who also died after a few months, and the romance of Crispi's life was ended. From that day until the declaration of Italian unity in 1860, his existence was that of a conspirator, in exile and poverty, accepting no occupation which restricted his liberty to change conspiracy to insurrection, and living with his eyes always turned towards Sicily. He has never loved another woman, though the irregular relations with the sex which are almost universal amongst his Italian contemporaries, have been unusually disastrous to him. A lady who knew him well at Turin, told me that he was always absolutely

indifferent to women, although they used to
"throw themselves at him." He has a
daughter by his later marriage, to whom,
and to Italy, he has given the absolute
devotion of his maturer life.

He practised at the bar of Palermo until
the age of twenty-three, when, according to
the decision of his father, he made the formal
application to be admitted to the magistracy,
and, although he still lacked two years to the
legal age for the entry into the lower grade,
he passed a brilliant examination, and the
authorities were easily induced to overlook
the deficiency of his years. According to the
law, he was required to spend three years
in a course of instruction under a superior
magistrate, and he was placed with Filippo
Craxi, procureur-general of the Court of
Cassation of Palermo. Beyond the functions
of this office, Craxi was charged with the
presidency of the commission for the exaction
of overdue taxes, and in the questions arising
from the execution of this office, the political
convictions of the young magistrate found
their expression, which decided him in the
abandonment of the imposed career. One of
the Sicilian magnates, the Prince of Castel-
nuovo, a rigid constitutionalist, had refused,
after the abolition by decree of the Sicilian
Parliament, to pay any taxes, on the ground
that taxation without the vote of the Parlia-

ment was illegal. Crispi sympathised with the Prince; his chief with the pretensions of Divine Right to impose on the subject whatever burthens it saw fit; and in the discussions which grew out of the case, the conviction seems to have established itself on Crispi that he could not serve the King, and he abandoned the magistrature, deciding on that course with the rapidity and firmness which have always marked his action in important junctures, and, finding the field of activity offered him in Palermo too limited, determined to go to Naples and enter at the bar.

He reached the capital without recommendations or influential acquaintances. The admission to the bar of Palermo was no qualification for that of Naples, so complete, in spite of the formal union of the two kingdoms, was their real separation. Sicily had always maintained a higher level of political and even civil condition—the assertion of independence, however unsuccessful, of the island population was never quite crushed, and an opportunity to breathe the air of freedom and constitutional institutions was never lost. What in Naples was only chafing at restraint, was in Sicily the assertion of old and unforgotten rights; and of all the Italian lands Sicily has always been the greatest centre of revolutionary activity. There was no sentiment in common until the idea of the common mother, Italy, was recognised by both. A Sicilian was a foreigner in Naples, and Crispi had to make his way as one. But the necessity of submitting himself to the primary steps of the preliminary examination of a young advocate, after his two years of practice at Palermo and his brilliant examination for admission to the bench, seemed derisory, and he declined to submit to it. He addressed himself to the procureur-general, Paolo Cumbo, to obtain for him the exemption from this, to him, rather humiliating formality, but only met a rebuff, the formality being considered obligatory to Neapolitans, much more to foreigners. He went further and applied to the Minister Parisio. Here he was met, the minister recognising the abilities of the young man, not by a refusal to the bar, but by a solicitation to return to the magistracy, but there had been in Palermo no reason for sacrificing his independence which did not equally exist at Naples, and he firmly refused though promised a rapid advancement, and the minister yielded to his insistence, and he was admitted to the bar without examination.

In the Neapolitan procedure in certain cases of administrative appeal the last word was pronounced by the King, and it was necessary for an advocate to be at least on friendly terms with the Court, a harder task for the embryo

republican than that of conciliating a tribunal,
but he at least succeeded professionally, the
King being, as Crispi has always maintained,
a just man in spite of his political education in
the straitest sect of despotism and contempt of
popular rights.   The Bourbon could only reign,
he never learned the secret of good government.
Crispi's liberal sympathies were not weakened
by the conditions of his career, and there were
not wanting occasions when he could make
them effective.   About 1845 the Sicilian village
of Belmonte, near Palermo, was the scene
of a political assassination, the victim being a
functionary of police.   The general who commanded at Palermo, Vial, proceeded to arrest
entire families of those accused—old men,
women, and children—and banished them
en masse.   Amongst the victims of this blind
rigour was the father of a young friend of Crispi,
a colleague at the bar, who flew to Naples and
demanded the help of Francesco.   The political
prosecutions cared little about forms of law,
the effectiveness of the repression being all
that was thought of, and no process of law had
any force against the military authority.   The
only help was in the King and a fortunate
presentation of the case to the Royal consideration.   Amongst the friends whom Crispi's
liberal tendencies had obtained him was
Marchese Ruffo, the minister of the Two
Sicilies at Florence, and through him he

obtained an audience for his friend at one of the more select receptions accorded to the favoured, at which the company were ranged round the hall of audience, as is now the custom at the Quirinal, the King entering from his cabinet and passing along the line, addressing a few words to each of the presented in turn, listening with affability to all complaints, and accepting all the petitions directly. Crispi had instructed his friend in what to say, to ask firstly the liberty to tell his whole story, then to ask the King to examine the affair himself. The hearing was given, and two days after orders were given to recall the banished families and to hasten the trial. On another occasion Crispi had to defend a commune in the vicinity of Messina against the pretensions of the arch-bishop. He obtained an audience and began to state his case, when the King interrupted him and finished the story. Crispi said, " I see that your Majesty knows the facts com-pletely ; will he permit me to state the law of the case ? " The King heard the law, thought it over and decided in favour of Crispi's clients.

Crispi has always rendered justice to the amiable personal qualities of the King, who, had he been otherwise educated, might have been the founder of the unity of Italy. But he was apathetic, good-natured, and only hated change of any kind that compelled him to move. Somebody reproached him with being indifferent to the great question of Italy, and quoted the example of Carlo Alberto of Sardinia. Ferdinand replied that "the King of Sardinia may begin his crusade for the unity of Italy when he likes, he will only meet at last the supreme obstacle, the Papacy ; it is not so for me, I shall meet it in the beginning," in which he showed the shrewdness of a politician if not the ambition of a king. He was a cynic and a pessimist, a kind-hearted man who did not care to find occasions to try his heart, and who would govern mildly so long as the people would be docile, but who entertained no question of limits to divine rights. He had no faith in honesty, and when he was told one day that the syndic of Naples was poor, he said to him, "What ! you are syndic of Naples two years and still poor !" When, on the eve of being deposed, he yielded and granted the constitution, he said, "What I have been spending for troops I will spend on the deputies." He despised the Neapolitans but feared the Sicilians, whose restless activity was always a menace to his repose, and whom he attempted to keep down in the only way he could trouble himself to try or conceive to be effective—by bayonets.

The intellectual life of Naples was at this time more vigorous in relation to the rest of Italy than now. It was the capital of a kingdom whose comparative importance in Italy we now forget, and drew to it the flower of what intellectual life the corrupted church and the pestilential influences of unmitigated despotism allowed to exist, of all that its intellect produced, for the Papal States were more stifling ; Tuscany less inviting as a field of activity for the ambitious ; and Piedmont was a foreign state, with which the Neapolitan had less sympathy than even with the Sicilian. We can hardly now appreciate the change between the condition of the peninsula, divided into states separated by every tradition of government or revolt against government, as foreign to each other as if there were no community of language or history, and without the even incomplete assimilation between provinces widely separated, which we now recognise. At the time that young Crispi entered on his career, Naples was the most brilliant centre of political activity in Italy, though everywhere in the peninsula there was the beginning of the great ferment which was to make the state. Tuscany, better governed, had not the same causes of discontent, and the Piedmontese monarchy, equally despotic, and scarcely more Italian, kept an effective control of the revolutionary tendencies by the profounder loyalty of the people. The warmer southern temperament brought the seeds of the doctrines of liberty planted by Mazzini, Gioberti, Tommasseo,

Mamiani, and their northern colleagues to a
quicker germination, if a less robust growth.
In 1843 began an agitation in the kingdom of
the two Sicilies, which had for its immediate
object the formation of a community of feeling
and action in the two still separate countries.
These had only lately been shut into the same
strong box of absolute rule, and Sicily was in
revolt as much against her loss of nationality as
against the abolition of her constitution and
liberties.   The committee which directed this
movement was composed of Mariano d'Ayala,
the brothers Assanti, Marchese Ruffo, and
Crispi, Sicilians ; Giovanni Raffaelle, a physi-
cian, and friend of Crispi and his god-father
in the movement, Bozzelli, Carlo Poerio, and
other Neapolitans.   Their first work was to
mitigate the race hostility between the two
kingdoms, for the subjection of Sicily to
Naples was not only the offence of the
Bourbons, but of all Neapolitans, by implica-
tion.   Sicily had been left in neglect, and under
rigours of government which perhaps the fiery
and indomitable character of the islanders made
necessary in a system of government like that
of the Bourbons, but which embittered them
against even their fellow-sufferers on the
mainland, and the jealousy was the greatest
obstacle to the necessary unity of action.
These causes of separation and paralysis were
not removed by the earlier movements, and

perhaps had much to do with the failure of them.

The Siculo-Neapolitan revolutionary committee could not long escape the notice of the police in a country where every element of government was made subordinate to the system of espionage, and the public funds were most readily expended for treachery. Spies got admission, the leading members were all denounced to the chief of Police, and all the plans were reported day by day. When the insurrection of Cosenza, on the 15th of March 1844, broke out, the chiefs were arrested, but it chanced that Crispi, being a stranger to Calabria and having taken no part in the preparations for this rising, was not denounced or arrested. His work was mainly in preparing the Sicilians for the hoped-for co-operation with the Neapolitan committee, and for this purpose he made frequent journeys to the island, as his profession, and especially his speciality of pleading cases for Sicilians in the courts of Naples, enabled him to do without exciting suspicion. When Pius IX. came to the papal throne, the liberalism of Italy and especially of Naples received a new stimulus, and Ferdinand II. fulminated against him as a Jacobin and Freemason endowed with all the qualities a good absolutist must detest, with the natural consequence that he became the hope of the Neapolitan liberals, as well as of

other dreamers of Italy. In the latter part of
1847 the Neapolitan movement, ill restrained
by the arrests of the principal members of the
committee, broke into manifestation in Naples,
by the publication of the "protest of the
people of the Two Sicilies," in which Luigi
Settembrini and Raffaelle, the sponsor of Crispi,
had been the most prominent workers ; and in
Messina by an insurrection on the 1st of September, with the watchwords " Long live Pius IX.,
Italy, and the Constitution." On the same day
the people in Reggio of Calabria rose, followed
by Gerace. Messina was quickly put down
and Reggio only resisted three days, to be
followed by Gerace, and the repression was
after the Bourbon taste. The Neapolitan
police arrested Poerio, d'Ayala, Domenico
Mauro, Francesco Trinchera, Baron Stocco,
and Marsino Cozzolini. Crispi was indicated
for arrest but owed his escape to a chance. In
the same house where he had his lodgings
lived a police agent and some officers of the
navy. Opposite dwelt a woman of easy virtue,
the beautiful mistress of the commissary of
police of the quarter, to whom the order to
arrest Crispi had been given. The commissary
delayed his duty in his dalliance, and the son
of the mistress, who was employed in the
printing office at which Crispi had his legal
documents printed, being one day too far in
wine to contain so important an item of infor-

mation from his companions, betrayed the plan. The head of the printing office made a pretext to call on Crispi and warned him that his arrest was impending, so that he had time to burn all compromising papers and warn his fellow - conspirators not to visit him ; and when the commissary came he not only found no reason to arrest Crispi, but even made a favourable report of him, which served for a long time to avert the attention of the police.

The Sicilian preparations continued, in spite of the repression of the partial movements of November, in Naples and Palermo, and in the latter part of December Crispi went to Palermo to prepare the great rising, which was fixed for the 12th of January 1848. All being ready he returned to Naples to inform the committee, and having seen the imprisoned conspirators, he set out to return for the rising at Palermo. In those days communication was precarious, and no vessel sailed from Naples for Palermo on the 11th or 12th. But if Crispi had no steamer, the King had no telegraph, and the anxiety of one was not felt by the other. On the 13th Crispi sailed, and landed on the second day of the fighting. He found the city in the power of the people, who exercised the most brutal vengeance on the police, the troops having retired to the fortress after the first day's fighting. The insurrection was something *sui generis* ;—the intention was known to

all the world of Palermo, and the night of the
11th of January was spent in preparations for
fighting on the next day, which, being the
birthday of the King, was a regularly observed
holiday ; the royal salutes opened the ball, for
the call to arms followed immediately. The
women took their places in the distribution
of colours and cockades, the priests exhorted
the people to rise, and harangued them in
the squares. Giuseppe La Masa, an exile just
returned, was called to the command, and the
bells rang out their alarm all over Palermo.
A detachment of cavalry fell into an ambuscade
and lost two men, on which they turned bridle
and escaped, throwing the other troops into a
panic ; and, at the end of the day, the troops
had ten killed, the people two, and that night
both sides rested on their arms, the people in
the open squares, while a committee was formed
to provide for the contest. There were but
forty muskets amongst them, but the city was
illuminated and the crowd went through the
streets shouting for liberty, Sicily, and Pius IX !
The next day the villages around sent in their
contingents of combatants, arms, and ammunition, and while the royal troops hesitated and
sent semaphoric messages to Naples for help,
the people organised, and before night had
three hundred muskets at their command.
The military retired to the citadel and opened
fire on the city, to which the insurgents replied

with an old cannon they had got, bound round with ropes to prevent it from bursting, and which made only a report which persuaded the troops that they had a battery. One battalion passed over to the insurrection. On the 14th Crispi arrived, and the provisional government was formed, barricades thrown up and special committees formed for the various needs of the movement—that for the army and navy being presided over by the Prince of Pantellaria with Crispi as secretary. After twenty-four days of active hostilities the forts capitulated.

In the work of the organisation which followed,—of an army sufficient to meet the forces which the King was sure to send from Naples,—Crispi had the larger part. The Parliament which was created included him amongst the deputies, and his uncle, Monsignor Crispi, bishop of Lampsacus and Sygea, presided over the Upper Chamber. The political tendencies Crispi then showed are those to which he has adhered all his life. He sat in the extreme Left, and when the article of the constitution which declared the religion of the state to be the Catholic, Apostolic, and Roman was discussed, he opposed any declaration on the subject of religion, it being arrogant to impose a faith. He proposed the formula declaring the King culpable of high treason, in place of that which simply deposed him, but

only on condition that he should employ force
to subjugate the nation. In the discussions
which followed the organisation of the Parliament, and which involved the principles of
constitutional liberty, Crispi showed in a remarkable degree a combination of foresight as
to the dangers of the position and prudence in
the advocacy of measures which might prevent
wise compromises and a reconciliation with
the throne. There was no question of the
republic, it was not in the traditions of Sicily,
but when the Bourbon King was found to be
irreconcilable the son of the King of Sardinia
Alberto-Amedeo was elected King.

Meanwhile the Bourbon King had been
preparing in silence for the reduction to obedi-
ence of the island. The English and French
Governments had practically recognised the
Sicilian independence and saluted the national
flag on the day when the Sicilian King was
declared, but the recognition was only platonic,
for when the Neapolitan army entered the
island, and it became a practical question if
Sicily should be supported or not, the eternal
jealousies broke out between the two Governments, and while France was inert, fearing
that Sicily, as having been at one time in
the past greatly under the English influence,
would be an instrument in the hands of that
power, Palmerston advised the reconciliation
of the island with the kingdom of Naples and

the *status quo*, with plenty of good counsels as
to concessions to be made, no doubt, though
no one hoped that any would be made except
under the compulsion of *force majeure* ; the two
Governments having agreed to abandon Sicily
to its fate if this were refused.   Sicily refused
it.   The Parliament which was inaugurated
with such enthusiasm on the 25th of March
1848 was prorogued on the 17th of April
1849, as the Neapolitan army was marching
on Palermo.   It had landed, 24,000 strong, at
Messina, the citadel of which city had always
been held by the royal troops, and after a siege
of eight days, the city, reduced to ruins by the
bombardment, surrendered.   The Neapolitan
army, commanded by Filangieri, moved slowly
westward, Milazzo, Barcelona, and the intervening towns along the north coast being
taken one by one, the war on the part of the
Sicilians seeming purely defensive, as if they
hoped that some just and humane intervention
of the powers would arrest the Neapolitans.

While Filangieri marched, conquering in
detail the small forces of the local defence, the
Sicilians were debating, hoping, and listening
to the persuasions of Admiral Baudin, sent by
the French Government to induce the island
to give over its resistance.   He brought no
positive engagements, but excited many ex-
pectations, in which the Sicilians shared more
or less as they knew little or much of the

King.   There was a want of unity and initiative on the part of the islanders, and they adopted the fatal policy of a passive defence, in the hope that Europe would see that they were righted.   The military forces of the island were sufficient to have driven Filangieri into the sea, had they been led by a man of resolution, supported by a Government with a definite plan ; but the Government was disconcerted, the most of the deputies timid, after the long, undecided struggle, so different in its results from what the anticipations of a year before had painted them, and instead of collecting the troops in various parts of the island, and attempting a vigorous defence by direct attack, the detachments were allowed to remain in garrison, waiting on events.   Dissensions arose, the authorities, by their indecision and vacillation slowly sapping the courage of those who desired to act, and who only waited for orders ; the bourgeoisie wanted to secure their material interests, and the general impression grew that there was no sortie from the difficulty except in a submission, which the veiled promises of the French admiral of concessions and amnesty made easier ; the committee even refused the arms and ammunition that were sent to carry on the struggle with, and in effect the end came for want of vitality in the movement, more than from want of courage.   But it came.

CHAPTER II

On the 20th of April the Neapolitan army was at the gates of Palermo. Such deputies and senators as still were willing to assume responsibility met at the house of the Marquis of Torrearsa to decide what was to be done—fight or surrender ; Crispi being for fighting. But in the night fear gained ground amongst the members of Parliament, and many went on shipboard, others into the interior, where there were still garrisons in a state of defence. On the 22nd Ruggiero Settimo, who had been the head of the Government, abdicated, and on the 25th embarked, and a few days later the Neapolitan army entered Palermo, having previously issued a proclamation promising an amnesty to all Sicilians except forty-three, amongst whom was Crispi, whom Filangieri had in one of his earlier despatches denounced as the most dangerous of the enemies of the King. The promise was utterly disregarded, and the prisons were filled with the insurgents, while numbers escaped to France, Italy, and Malta. Crispi remained in hiding till the

7th, when he embarked with Rosolino Pilo and the brothers Orlando, all of whom we shall find later in history associated again with him.

Landing at Marseilles, he went by land to Turin. Here he addressed himself to that *dernier résort* of intellect in difficulties, of ambition with talent, and of the patriot and philanthropist with a purpose—journalism, uniting all these motives in his resolutions. It was the opening of the career which never rested or accepted any solatium until, in 1860, he finally saw his native island free and united to Italy, as he had always determined, as far as in him lay, it should be. When, in the Sicilian Parliament, he had discussed the organisation of the island, it was always with the distinct and expressed provision that it was to be Italian, a part of the mother-land, and in this faith he laboured in whatever way his hands found open to him. He took a place on the staff of a democratic journal, *La Concordia*, conducted by Lorenzo Valerio, and remained on it till Cesare Correnti founded the *Progresso*, then the journal which was, in what pertained to style and correctness of management, at the head of Italian journalism, as Correnti was at the head of journalists, and even of conspirators. He had taken part in the organisation of the Five days of Milan, and in the most important movements of the

brilliant failure of the Italian awakening of
1848-9. On the staff of the *Progresso* with
Crispi were Depretis and Seismit-Doda, afterwards his colleagues in the ministry. The
Italian press is, even to-day, probably the
worst paid and the most feebly supported of
all Europe, and in those days was evidently
much worse off, for the pay of Correnti, then
reckoned one of the most polished writers of
Italian, was, for writing the leading articles,
90 francs a month. Depretis, who wrote the
reports of the Parliament, had the same, and
Crispi, as administrator and chronicler, with
the charge of the minor matters, had 60 francs
a month. But he also wrote for the *Corriere
di Milano*, the *Gazzetta di Torino*, the *Archivio
Storico*, and the *Panteone dei Martiri della
Libertá Italiana*, besides writing studies on
various political topics for future use and
elaborating his conceptions of government for
when he should be called, as his spirit told
him he should be some day, to help govern
the country he was labouring to form.
Amongst the papers which then gave expression to his nervous activity and febrile passion
of production is a memoir on the last events
of the Sicilian Revolution, dated 20th December 1849, a cold, impartial, at times
sarcastic, analysis of the causes of the failure
of the movement and the part England and
France had taken in it, evidently written under

the influence of the emotions of the day after
the event, when the passion has subsided, and
when one sees more clearly and understands
many things which at first were puzzles. He
says there that Louis Napoleon, in July 1848,
proposed himself as King of Sicily, and gives
in detail the promises of a constitution and an
independent Sicilian Government, made by the
representatives of the French Government, and
which so much weakened the resistance of the
Sicilian population and caused division in their
councils. The document is confused, as if
there was too much to be said, and the ideas
crowded themselves too fast on the mind of
the writer to be put in order, but the tone is
dispassionate and didactic, as a history of events
almost forgotten, and reminds one of Crispi's
manner in the Chamber of Deputies when
discussing a law. One can imagine him saying
to himself as he wrote it : " This shall be
put on record for the times when Sicilians can
understand their history and the cause of their
misfortunes ; this shall serve to render justice
to those who suffered, as to those who did, the
wrongs. Whatever may happen to me, the
real causes of the failure of the insurrection of
Sicily in 1848 shall be known in all their
bareness, and the lesson stand for good." He
says not a word of himself or the measures he
urged, the policy he advocated—the whole
story is told as one might tell it who looked

on and understood the secret springs of action of all the participators.

There does not exist, so far as I can learn, a document by him of this time which betrays impatience or resentment. His life of hard work and severe temperance strengthened the natural gravity of his temperament, and he had a future to think of which obscured the dreary present and the sadder past. In his garret at the top of a lodging - house, he received his colleagues of the *Progresso*, combining their frugal provision for supper, one bringing the bread, another the cheese or whatever he had to contribute—on sixty francs a month, one does not frequent the restaurants much, as we know who have tried it. One of the comrades of these entertainments, Revere, an occasional contributor to the journal, has left this record of Crispi as he then was : " He was a republican and did not conceal it, republican by temperament, reason, and conviction, without ostentation or tendency to make converts. He spoke little, and never told all that he thought. With all that, he was proud, thoughtful, settled in his ideas, incapable of any compromise with his conscience or his principles. It was proposed to Crispi, to write on liberal terms for the *Risorgimento*, a journal of moderate - liberal opinions founded by Count Cavour. He replied indignantly ' Do you think that a

publicist is like a shoemaker who makes shoes
for all feet ? ' " He refused to write for
Cavour, because his principles were opposed
to those of the Count, but he did not hold
his republicanism so severely that he could
not accept a half-way measure when the whole
was unattainable, as he voted for the Duke
of Genoa for King of Sicily in 1848, and as
subsequently, and at a far more important
period of his life, and when his action was
in a measure decisive of the shape of Italian
institutions, he saw that the Republic in the
hands of Italian republicans meant the revival
of the divided state, the old provincial lines
redrawn, and Italian unity inevitably abolished
in favour of a new scheme of federation of
the old states under new and untried conditions
of government, he went over to the Monarchy
with his memorable saying, which has been
the watchword of Italian unitarian politics
ever since, " The Monarchy unites us, the
Republic would divide us."

Crispi's condition must have been intolerable at this time, for he was willing to abandon
journalism for the wretched position of communal secretary to a little village of Piedmont,
Verolengo, where a vacancy had occurred.
What the stipend was, I do not know, but no
position of that kind in Italy gives more than
a bare living to a frugal man, and this little
mountain village could not have offered more

E

than fifty or sixty pounds a year. The following is the letter in which he asks for the appointment :—

Mr., the Syndic—Imperious circumstances which it is useless to describe here, hinder me from coming to your commune to present myself to you and the honourable members of the communal council of Verolengo. Nevertheless, you will find in my memoir and the documents I enclose, the indications of the qualities I possess. I believe that you will with difficulty find amongst my competitors the recommendations I offer. It is a singular thing—it must be attributed to the exceptional position in which I have been thrown by the events of 1848— that a man who has held elevated positions, who has been advocate at the Court of Appeal of the most populous city of Italy, should present himself as candidate for a position as communal secretary. This fact is itself my recommendation. My request indicates the manner in which I wish to employ the leisure which political changes have brought on me ; in giving my studies and my labour to the commune which you so worthily administer, and gaining honourably my bread by my work.

I do not come to you with letters of recommendation, which would be an affront to me and to the distinguished citizens who would honour me by their votes. My recommendations can be justly estimated without the authority of great names. In its good sense, the municipal council has no need to be prompted to do what it ought.

Would you be so courteous as to read this letter to the Council, and believe me your very devoted servant, Advocate F. CRISPI-GENOVA.

The custom in Sicily then was (and to a certain extent still is) to add the name of the mother to that of the father, and Crispi's mother was of the family Genova.

One wonders if any of the municipal counsellors of Verolengo, in the years that have followed, ever learned that the last of the line of the great makers of Italy had begged for the poor place of secretary to his council; and one can but think what must have been his straits, with his unfaltering confidence in his future and his sense of his abilities (for he has never wavered in an estimate of himself and his political destinies which approaches arrogance) to induce him, so proud by nature, to ask for a place in the humble language of a servant, but which yet betrays his independence in refusing to ask for recommendations which no doubt he could have had from his friends in Turin, could he have bent himself to ask and disclose his needs. He was then a man of thirty, and had only to accept the place on the journal of Cavour to secure his position, financially and politically, for Cavour recognised his abilities and his inflexibility as well; but we are asked to believe that in later times he has lost his independence and his honesty together !

But harder things were in store for the Sicilian exile. Mazzini, in the spring of 1853 attempted to raise an insurrection in Lombardy.

The ground was ill prepared, and most of the revolutionary chiefs were opposed to the undertaking. Kossuth, who was preparing a movement in Hungary, which in the original plan of the movement was to be simultaneous with the rising in Lombardy, was unable to make his preparations in time to act with Mazzini, and attempted to dissuade him from it ; but as Mazzini persisted, fearing that his hold on the insurrectional element was being weakened by the long inaction, Kossuth sent orders to the Hungarian regiments in Milan not to fire on the people if they rose. This was all he could do, for, as he said at the time to me, " I cannot play with the blood of my people." Of course the insurrection failed as had been foreseen, but while Mazzini, who was in Milan at the rising, escaped, all the leading republicans in Turin were arrested, suspected of complicity, and amongst them was Crispi. In prison he made the acquaintance of Agostino Bertani. The police found nothing to charge Crispi with, but he was exiled from the Sardinian kingdom, and went to Malta, where he founded a journal, the *Valigia*, which afterwards became the *Staffetta*, a paper naturally of advanced liberal sentiments. He lived for a time at Valetta, but afterwards took a cottage in a little village near the town. Mayor (*Revue Internationale*, 1890-91) gives an incident of this sojourn which shows that he never lost his faith in the

coming unity of Italy.   He contracted a friendship for the Sardinian consul at Malta, to whom
he foretold that he would be one day consul
for that Italy which as yet had only existenee
in the dreams of her children.   But even
Malta was disturbed by his presence and his
active correspondence with the other Italian
refugees, and he was again driven out on his
wanderings.   An English man-of-war gave him
passage to London ;   here he made the personal
acquaintance of Mazzini, with whom he had
long corresponded but whom he had never
met.   For Mazzini Crispi had, and always
retains, the most profound reverence and
affection, as the Apostle of Italy and Liberty,
the man who never faltered or lost his faith in
the success of his mission, and who, if he was
often mistaken in his choice of means, was
never selfish or mistaken in the ultimate result
he aimed at.   Both were republicans, and both
desired the unity of Italy—if in the later phase
of the development of the unity they differed
as to details of action, at this time there was
no difference, liberty being the first step, after
which the form would come.   To rid Italy of
the incubus of foreign intervention was the
first condition of any Italian government, and
Mazzini was ready to accept any means, and,
in spite of all the denials of his friends in later
days, I am satisfied that even regicide was to
him an acceptable instrument of coercion.   He

did not hesitate to provoke insurrection when, if he was as wise as we believe him, he must have known that the only result would be to make martyrs, and water the tree of Liberty with the blood of her worshippers ; and why should the blood of a tyrant who made the sacrifices imperative be more sacred ? But at this time, in the year of our Lord 1853, the prospects of freedom were so dark that even men who hesitated about shedding blood by private sanction might well be pardoned if they accepted the murder of a wholesale murderer of nations as a righteous sacrifice. The horrible suppressions in Hungary, after 1849, the slaughter of Paris in 1852, the tortures of Cayenne, and the great crimes against human rights of the later French empire, seemed enough to justify the execution of a tyrant on the individual responsibility of a man who believed that he was the heaven-appointed liberator of his compatriots. Mazzini ordered an insurrection as a general ordered an attack ; it mattered not if it succeeded so long as it was a part of a comprehensive plan which in the end must succeed. The insurrection of Milan of 1853 was of this nature—but Mazzini was no general, but a theorist and enthusiast, blindly confident in his own judgment—there was no hope of success, and so Kossuth had solemnly declared when Mazzini communicated his plans for the Milanese rising ;

but the Italian replied that it was necessary to do something to keep up his authority—the fire must be kept up. In this manner of thinking Crispi did not agree with him—the theory of liberty had always to yield to the prospects of success, and he took no part in the movement of Milan, though probably in full possession of the plan. In Sicily he had been one of the most sanguine and the most obstinate to hold out when all hope seemed gone, because he had not then learned the futility and falsity of diplomacy ; and when the English and French Governments had recognised the justice and success of the movement, and the ancient kingdom of Sicily was set on its legitimate basis, he had the naïveté to suppose that the official action of those governments would follow the lines of their diplomacy ; but in this, as in later movements, he looked to their practical solution and took no part in those which promised none. But, Sicilian above all, he waited and planned for Italy, and during his exile in England, while he studied English, he sought any occupation by which he could support himself, for the pittance his father could allow him was not enough to keep soul and body together. He gave lessons, he kept the books of a countryman in business who profited by his necessities and helplessness in a strange land, but after a year of struggle which left him in debt, he decided to go to Paris, where at least he was at home in the language, and where a compatriot, Giacinto Carini, who managed the *Courrier Franco-Italien* had invited him to assist in the management. The liberality of his chief being in default, in spite of his previous urgent invitations, Crispi accepted a position in a bank, kept by a Parisian whom Mazzini believed to be a confederate and fellow-conspirator, but who was really an intriguant who made use of Mazzini's friendship and made no return. This engagement ended, like the others, in disappointment, and the exile had, like so many others, to live by chance labour, writing for the journals, frequenting the society of the members of the bar, and gaining a bare livelihood. He kept up his relations with Mazzini, and was the channel through which many of his documents were circulated, but he was never implicated in any local movement. In 1856 he was arrested but found guiltless of any offence and remained unmolested until the attempt of Orsini, when all the Italians in Paris, and Crispi amongst them, were arrested. The rigorous perquisition to which he was subjected discovered nothing incendiary or compromising amongst his papers or effects, and after a detention of a few hours and a thorough searching of his papers, he was released. His habit of seclusion and study which kept him at home through the evenings served him in good stead, for the investigation dispelled all the preventions of the police against him as Italian, and in fact he had never held any relations with the conspirators against the French Government, unless the dissemination of the proclamations sent him by Mazzini could be called such. He dreamed of his native Sicily, and his plans for her were the basis of the hopes for Italy. Where indeed should he have hoped more for the beginning of the regeneration ? The proud, high-spirited island, accustomed to the constitutional regime when all Italy beside was under absolutism, innoculated with the English ideas of government during the occupation of the Napoleonic wars, alone of the Italian provinces never subjected to the French rule, and preserving all its strong individuality therefore as none other had, sensitive as to the preservation of its ancient privileges and laws, was then the point at which the movement for Italian emancipation would most rationally and easily commence ; and this was always in the mind of Crispi, to whom his country was the *pou sto* of the liberator.

And in the revolutionary evolution this was the natural order. Sicily had always been the kindling point of insurrection and the refuge of constitutional forms in Italy, and if it were only a question of popular revolt, the island was the natural spring of agitation.

From Sicily to Naples was but a passage, and
Naples, so far from Austria and so important
to England under the old state of things, was
at all times ready for a movement.   Then
Crispi's experience of north-Italian freedom,
the domination of the Piedmontese system and
ruling class, exclusive in their own privilege
of emancipation, as if Italy were only and
finally to be annexed to the sub-Alpine state
and not be Italy but a great Piedmont ; all this
made the plans of northern conspirators of less
interest to a Sicilian, and still less did he
interest himself in the plotting of French republicans.   He laboured to establish himself
in Paris, to make a position at the bar, and to
wait there for the day when Sicily should
renew the struggle.   But his hard fortune
followed him still.   In August 1858 he
received an order to leave France in forty-eight
hours.   He had friends who did what was
possible to obtain the revocation of the order,
but all in vain, he was obliged to leave for
England, the only European state then open
to him.

Mayor tells an incident of this expulsion
which is interesting as an example of the
manner in which Crispi has always inspired
confidence in those who have to deal with him.
He had only shortly before purchased the
furniture of his apartment on the system of
periodical payments, and had only half paid for

it.   He went to his creditor and telling him
that he was exiled again, and that he could not
pay what was owing, proposed to him to take
the furniture and so cancel the debt. Megissot,
the furniture dealer, replied, "I will do nothing
of the kind, you are expelled from France ;
this is a misfortune which I regret, but you
are an honest man. The furniture you have
purchased is yours, even if you have not
finished the payments. Take it with you, it
is your right ; you will pay me when you can."
And Crispi did not succeed in moving him
from his resolution.   He went to London
again, and there he suffered the old deprivations
and was unable to pay the remnant of the
debt.   Then came 1859 and the movements
in Italy ; 1860 and the expedition of Marsala,
and it was only in 1862 that Crispi began to
improve his situation by the exercise of his
profession and was the master of his fortunes
again.   He revisited Paris, and the first visit
he made was to the furniture dealer.   "Do
you know me, Monsieur Megissot ?" he said.
"Do I know you, indeed ?   Certainly I know
you.   I know whom I trust, Monsieur Crispi.
I have followed your career, applauded your
successes, and it is as much as your friend as
your creditor that I am glad to see you again."

Crispi was still in London when the propositions of Napoleon III. to Cavour brought
the emancipation of Italy again into the field

of practical politics. The Italian exiles, united in London, drew up a manifesto against the treaty with the Emperor, and declared that they would take no part in any war against Austria under such auspices. The document was drawn up by Mazzini, and bears, amongst its signatures, that of Crispi. It says:

" The war, if carried on under the plans and with the alliance of Louis Napoleon Bonaparte, cannot have for object and result the unity of Italy, which is opposed, and obnoxious, to his ambitious designs, and declared by him impossible.

" To provoke insurrection in, and make war for, a single fraction of Italy, leaving the other portions dismembered prey to the tyranny of the worst of governments, would be the forfeiture of honour, country, and our plighted faith, and betray at the same time the future. . . .

" We declare consequently that so far as the Piedmontese Monarchy is concerned, it is not a question with the exiled Italian of the Republic, but of unity and national sovereignty.

> . . . . .

" Abhorring equally the Austrian in Lombardy and every foreigner in Rome or any other point of Italy ; loving with the same affection the Italian of Sicily or the Italian of the Alps, we wish and ardently desire war, but not a war of slaves, not a war like those of the Middle Ages, against one stranger for the

advantage and profit of another ; not a war
for a fraction of Italy, a war of mere dynastic
aggrandisement, but a war of freemen, a war
for all, founded on a national principle held as
sacred in Europe—the war of a people which,
faithful to the traditions of its geniuses and its
martyrs, wishes to reconquer a country, a flag,
a common social pact."

CHAPTER III

THE war of 1859 ended, as the exiles had foreseen, in a compromise and a fraud practised on Italy by the Emperor. Italy lost Savoy and Nice, and was cheated out of Venice, but the agitation which it left in Italy, and the hopes raised and which no Imperial-Royal treaty or pacification could henceforth subdue, developed the determination on the part of the exiles to continue the work which the war had begun. They decided to return to Italy and agitate for the rejection of the conditions of the treaty of Villafranca and a continuance of the movement, Crispi, with his friends Rosolino Pilo and La Masa undertaking Sicily. Crispi left England with a passport in the name of Manuel Pareda, Argentine, disguised as a merchant; and by the way of Genoa, Civita Vecchia and Naples he finally landed at Messina. He has kept a minute diary of the voyage, which was sent by post at frequent intervals to London, both for security to himself and that the information should not be lost in case of his arrest. He at once renewed acquaintance with former

associates and began the organisation of a new
insurrection. He carried the method of manu-
facturing explosive bombs, Orsini bombs, they
were then called, and taught it as he went, for
the benefit of the people in the next rising.
At Palermo the plans were combined for the
insurrection, in which Palermo as usual was to
lead, and the part of each of the confederates
was arranged, and the date was fixed for the
4th of October following ; and to complete the
arrangements, obtain the arms and co-operation
from the mainland, with whatever other combinations might be found necessary, Crispi set
out on his return voyage. Reading his diary,
minute in all details of meetings and plan, one
is struck with the tone of security and conviction in the success of the scheme which prevails
in it all, as if no failure were possible, and not
a little with the confidence in which the visits
were made to so many compatriots, in the
assurance of the trustworthiness of so large a
part of the population as became aware of his
identity, as well as with the confidence he
seemed to inspire in his colleagues. But
reaching Florence, where all was then in the
provisional state of the months succeeding the
peace of Villafranca, with the dictature of
Farini at Modena and Ricasoli at Florence,
where Mazzini was in hiding, he finds it
necessary to continue to London, whence he
could operate in greater security than from

Italy, change his passport, identity, and take a
new departure, for his genius for conspiracy
never neglected the most insignificant precaution against discovery. He only remained
one day in Tuscany, and by way of Paris left
for England. At Genoa he received the
following letter from Mazzini, which it is
useful to quote since the impression has obtained that *he* was the organiser of the conspiracy which determined the Expedition of
The Thousand.

FRIEND—Listen ! If you arrive before—and if
they persist in the day—send me first a telegraphic
despatch which says : "the account has been paid,"
to Sig. Giovanni Lagrange, Lugano, Ticino, Switzer-
land. It is very important. Send it ten, five hours
before. If there is delay do not telegraph but write.

If there is no way of avoiding that they offer
themselves (the Sicilians to Piedmont) let it be done
with dignity, demanding acceptation unconditionally,
yes or no. If at that time he (the King) should have
given the customary reply to Parma, Modena,
Bologna, in truth it would be a pity to offer themselves. Then insist on the provisional government,
the declaration of belonging to Italy when Italy shall
be ; and send messages of fraternity to the Centre
etc., etc.

If the day should come in which they have no
fear of my secret stay, or if discovered, telegraph.

Your first telegram will give me means to send
people immediately ; some Italian soldiers, and some
Hungarians.

If there is occasion, write me as soon as you can a

letter in which you will give the particulars and tell me something of the tendencies of the men who shall have been elected—it is important.

Addio! I confess that I would be with you : but I will seek to aid you, urging immediately over there as you know. I think of Naples and do what I can there.—Entirely yours,   Gius.

16th September.

For the second voyage Crispi's faithful Maltese friend Tamajo, had procured him the passport of one Tobias Glivau, Maltese, of the age of forty-five, which was easily exchanged for a new and clean one from the Foreign Office. Before the day of starting Crispi received a telegram from Tamajo, saying that the day of the rising had been postponed to the 12th, signs of timidity already beginning to obtain. He left on the 6th *via* Paris, Marseilles, and by direct boat to Messina. Arriving at Messina he was met by the news that the friends have lost all desire to revolt, and that he is enjoined not to come there,— there is nothing ready and his presence might compromise everything, and that he must not even remain in Sicily but continue his voyage on the steamer which was destined for Peiraeus, etc. The few friends who came to see him on board showed that the panic had spread amongst the conspirators, and that the resolution which had responded to Crispi's faith and energy had evaporated with his departure.

F

He notes that all whom he met, whether of the Government party or not, seemed to apprehend a catastrophe as if the movements and the war in Upper Italy had shaken the foundations of the political organisation. He is not persuaded that his friends are right, and makes in his diary this comment. " All these things and others, spoken to me with trepidation, and as if by men who do not know what they want, give me the persuasion that even those who feel the necessity of action, fear to decide on it. The leaders of the national cause lack the force of mind necessary to men who must serve for example and guide. The revolution, mature in the country, and which a little spark might kindle, may delay long and perhaps be abortive."

Amongst so many apprehensions and in view of the inexplicable apathy of his confederates he could not persist in forcing on them a movement which they protested against, and he decided to go on to Greece. The diary of his stay at Athens shows his Philhellenic sympathies, but has no political interest otherwise, and is a *résumé* of the ordinary interested tourist, and his recollections of ancient history. On his return he stopped at Malta, where he learns that on the day last appointed for the rising, the 12th of October, a rising was attempted, but from the timidity of the men who ought to have been the leaders, or from the want of the one who might have given confidence to the rest, it was not seconded, and after three days' inefficient struggle it was suppressed entirely. From Malta he wrote to Mazzini two letters, in the first of which he gives a general account of the events and the condition of affairs, declaring his conviction that without the presence of men from the mainland there will be no possibility of raising the island successfully. In the second he discusses the general political situation at length, in which he shows that from Piedmont there had been letters written to the Sicilians to check any movement. Also from Malta he writes to the committee of Palermo to reproach them for their inaction and to show the importance of the action of the two Sicilies for the success of a general Italian movement. Arriving at Malta on the 29th of October, he was at once ordered to leave the island, and could only remain until the 6th of November, when the first steamer for Gibraltar sailed. Landing at Gibraltar, he travelled overland to Italy and went at once to Modena, where Luigi Carlo Farini was dictator of the new state of Emilia, of which Modena was capital.

Farini is described by Crispi in his diary, in the following terms:—"Farini is a true Romagnolo. A revolutionary nature, he is, amongst the moderates, the one who best comprehends the present situation of Italy."

Received at once by the dictator, he narrates
the experiences of his journeys and conspiracies,
the failure and the state of Sicily, and his conviction that with a little aid from without
they might throw off the yoke of the Bourbons.
Farini listened to the narration, and after thinking in silence over it, said " I am ready to help
you, and for my part, if it is a question of
money, I will give a million francs."   " The
money I accept," replied Crispi, " but it is not
enough.   I want something more."   " Say
what, then."   " Hear me," said Crispi ; " the
Government of Emilia had to send away the
body of volunteers which it feared would cross
the Catholica frontier.   I do not pass judgment
on the fact which irritated Garibaldi who,
disgusted, since November, has retired to
Caprera.   The volunteers disbanded are an
embarrassment to you.   I would find a way to
gather them together in the island of Elba,
and having formed a body of two thousand
men, I would promise at a given moment to
have them led by Garibaldi, and in two or
three steamers, conduct them to Sicily."   Farini
replied, " But for that project I could do nothing.
It would be necessary to obtain the co-operation of Commendatore Rattazzi and Baron
Ricasoli.   How do you stand with them ?"
" Rattazzi I knew in 1853 when I was expelled
from Piedmont.   For Ricasoli you must find
me a way."   " Very well.   I will give you a

letter for Col. Malenchini who is at Florence. Come to an understanding with him. He is an ardent patriot, can put you in communication with Baron Ricasoli, and can personally aid you in the execution of your project. To secure its success it is necessary above all that you go to Turin and that you come to an agreement with Rattazzi. If the Government of the King does not consider your enterprise opportune it is useless to persist, and I could do nothing for you." And Farini took a sheet of paper and wrote the following letter to Malenchini :

DEAR CENCIO—See and receive with confidence this gentleman, who will talk with you on important subjects. Having spoken with him, and with a few prudent and secret persons, we can then come to an understanding. Meanwhile I salute you—Your

FARINI.

The last entry of the diary is this— "December 10. I leave for Turin."

This was on the eve of the opening of the negotiations for the preparation of the expedition of The Thousand, the most splendid achievement of Young Italy, and the most brilliant success of Garibaldi.

The interview with Rattazzi led to nothing. Crispi again detailed his plans and hopes, Rattazzi accepting in principle, but making difficulties of the manner, called in La Farina, a Sicilian who had been one of the ministry of

Palermo in 1849, and with him Crispi had
to discuss anew the projected movement.   La
Farina, as was shown by subsequent events,
was a man of timid and narrow views, and
found objections to all that Crispi proposed.
The negotiations ended in nothing, and Rattazzi
finally refused what Crispi asked, which was
simply that the Sardinian ministry should see
nothing and give him the means for arming
his expedition.   Rattazzi fell, and Cavour
returned to office.   Enemy of all " Mazzinian "
plans and influences as Cavour was, his advent
to power dispelled the last hope of any assistance from the Government of the King, and
Crispi turned elsewhere for aid.   Put under
police surveillance in Turin, he at once went
to Genoa, where at that moment arrived his
friend and right hand, Rosolino Pilo, with
whom he set himself to finding new allies.
They appealed to Bertani, and he to Garibaldi,
and communicated their projects to him.   The
General promised that if the Sicilians rose, he
would aid them, adding, " In case of action,
remember that the programme must be, ' Italy
and Vittorio Emanuele.'"   In these negotiations
the winter passed and the time to begin operations had come.   Assured of the co-operation
of Garibaldi, the two Sicilians hesitated no
longer to commit themselves to the adventure,
and while Crispi remained to organise and
conduct the volunteers, Rosolino and another

Sicilian named Carrao hired a sailing craft, and
with such arms as they had and some money
provided by Mazzini, they landed at Messina.
They began with a misfortune ; Crispi's letter
to his correspondent at Messina found him in
prison, and no warning of their arrival had
been given to the confederates, but finding
that the insurrection had broken out in the
vicinity of Palermo, they decided to join it,
but only arrived to find that after a desperate
struggle the insurgents had been put to flight
and had dispersed into the mountains south of
Palermo, where Rosolino and his companions
joined them and kept up the insurrection in
the country. By the 7th of April the insurrection was known at Genoa, and Crispi,
Bertani, and Bixio met and decided to call on
Garibaldi for the fulfilment of his promise.
Garibaldi, nothing loath, asked a day's delay
for news from Palermo through Sir James
Hudson, English minister at Turin, and a
constant friend of Garibaldi and of Italian
liberty. The reply received through Sir James
being in accordance with the information of
Crispi, Garibaldi sent Bixio to Genoa to charter
a steamer, and Crispi to Milan to receive the
arms and money collected by the committee
which had been formed at the appeal of the
General for the purchase of a million rifles.
Most of the friends of the General dissuaded
him from the attempt ; the influences that beset

him were such that he was almost shaken in his resolution; Massimo d'Azeglio, then governor of Lombardy, confiscated the rifles, and even Farini, now become Minister of the Interior of the Sardinian kingdom, had changed his disposition. Volunteers flocked in and arms were got by stratagems which were not without danger, and the embarkation from Genoa was opposed by the authorities. The difficulties were very great, and probably the faith and tenacity of Crispi saved the expedition.

On the 2nd of May Garibaldi, harassed by the urgencies of his friends, and even of many friends of Italy who considered the undertaking certain to bring disaster on Italian liberation and worse to Sicily, hesitating, conferred with Crispi alone. Garibaldi said, " You are the only one who encourages me to undertake the expedition to Sicily; why? every one else discourages me." " If I do so," replied Crispi, " it is because I am convinced that it will be useful to our country and glorious for you. I have only one apprehension—the uncertainty of the sea." " I answer for the sea," replied the General. " And I for the land," said Crispi. The expedition was then practically determined. There was a cipher telegram received from Fabrizi at Malta, which, based on the news from Palermo, according to which the insurrection was at an end, and which, had it been credited by Garibaldi, would have possibly suspended the expedition, but Crispi had fuller information, according to which, and this was the truth, the insurrection was in vigour in the mountains, where Pilo and his band were in undisturbed possession, and the telegram was deciphered by the light of the direct information of Crispi. Fabrizi, at Malta, had knowledge of the city only, and there it was true that the insurrection was stifled. Crispi knew that the whole island was practically in insurrection, and only wanted a flag and a leader to rally round, and the flag and leader were secured. The question decided, no time was lost in making the preparations for the voyage, which Garibaldi assumed. He put Bixio in charge. The number of volunteers was less than had been hoped for; the arms were not in hand; the opposition of the officials was effective, and made it very difficult to operate; Cavour was silent, which was all that could be expected of him, and affected to know nothing, but his subordinates threw every obstacle in the way. On an old hulk in the harbour of Genoa, Bixio embarked the nucleus of the force, and when the moment came these boarded the two steamers, which, by the fiction of the circumstances, were to be supposed to be taken by force, and, having amongst their numbers the engineers, the pilots, and the crew necessary, the steamers

were at once ready to sail. The volunteers
were rapidly embarked and put to sea. But
arms were intercepted, and as those which the
men carried with them were insufficient for
the needs, some treachery having intervened,
the expedition promised failure on the thres-
hold. It had been arranged that the rifles,
etc., should be shipped on two barges, which
were to meet the steamers outside the port,
but they never appeared, and the steamers
steered for Quarto. Garibaldi had gone too
far to retreat, and knowing that, at Orbetello,
in the ancient Tuscan fortress, there was a
deposit of arms and ammunition, perhaps some
artillery as well, ordered the course to be
made for that place, and sent General Turr
with an order to the commander of the fortress
to give him all that he might require "for an
expedition that we are undertaking for the
glory of Piedmont and the grandeur of Italy."
The commander, Colonel Giorgini, doubtless
aware that he risked a court-martial and being
shot, yielded to the magic of the name of
Garibaldi, and allowed the expedition to take
the arms it needed.

The landing-point of the expedition had
not been decided, and in the consultation
between Garibaldi and those who did not
know the island, and Crispi who did, the
opinions differed. The pilot advised Trapani,
Garibaldi preferred Marsala, and Crispi a little

port on the south side of the island, Porto
Palo, where was no garrison or fortification.
Trapani was rejected for various reasons, and
the steamers held for Marsala, tentatively
doubtful whether the port might not be
occupied by the Neapolitan men-of-war. A
fishing-boat assured them of the presence of
two English steamers in the harbour and no
troops in the city, and the order for full speed
was given, and the landing effected in the
dramatic way that all the world knows, with
the arrival immediately after of the Neapolitan
squadron, the traditional English men-of-war in
the line of fire and preventing the royal ships
from firing on the volunteers as they went
ashore. There has never been any evidence of
an understanding having been arrived at between
Sir James Hudson and Garibaldi that the landing should be at Marsala, and the English
men-of war should be present at the landing
for all the contingencies that might arise.
Otherwise, it was said, why should Garibaldi,
who knew not a foot of the coast, insist on
Marsala against the opinions of the pilot and
of Crispi, who knew it well, and especially
Crispi, who had studied for this effect, and
who pointed out a spot where no interference
of the Neapolitan fleet was to be apprehended,
and from which the way to Palermo was at
least as short as from Marsala? Of course
the intervention of the English steamers is an

invention. As they had taken their anchorage before the arrival of the Neapolitan vessels, the latter had free choice of position and line of fire. It is probable that they feared the possible action of the English ships, and so delayed their own until too late. The English commander could not know where Garibaldi would decide to land, but Garibaldi was not the man to play the comedy of a council where he had already decided. Garibaldi ordered Crispi to land and take possession of the city. With a guard of fifty riflemen from Pavia, he took possession of the municipality, issued his orders to the functionaries, and prepared for the occupation of a day. Garibaldi sent a telegraphist to take the telegraph, with orders to reply to inquiries from Palermo whether there were any steamers in sight, that there were none, that the sea was calm, and then ordered the wires to be cut. The next morning began the march on Palermo, almost unanimously indicated by the staff, Crispi included, as the object of the first attack. Crispi was appointed assistant chief of staff, Sirtori being the chief, and the first night the army halted at the village of Rampagallo, where the first of the Sicilian bands joined them. The next day they arrived at Salemi, and here the real work of Crispi began, for here the organisation of the Government was decided on definitely. The Sicilians, Crispi, Carini,

La Masa, Castiglia, Orsini, and other notables counselled a dictature, and the proclamation of it was drawn up at Salemi by Crispi in the following terms :—

SALEMI, 14*th of May* 1860.

Italy and Victor Emmanuel.

Giuseppe Garibaldi, commander-in-chief of the national forces in Sicily ;

On the invitation of the notable citizens and the deliberations of the free communes of the island ;

Considering that in time of war it is necessary that the civil and military powers should be concentrated in one person ;

Decrees :

To assume, in the name of Vittorio Emanuele, King of Italy, the dictatorship in Sicily.

The Dictator—G. GARIBALDI.
F. CRISPI.

CHAPTER IV

THE story of the Revolution of 1860 is outside my limitations except as it involves Crispi in the narrative, and while all the members of the expedition were combatants by necessity, in face of the enormous superiority of the forces of the Bourbon Government, the services rendered by Crispi as sub-chief of staff, and the one best acquainted with the topography of the island from boyhood, became, after the taking of Palermo, entirely subordinate to those which he rendered as Secretary of State to the Dictator and as designer of all the political measures which were required to re-organise the island, thrown for the moment by the invasion and overthrow of the Bourbon Government into confusion. He took his part as combatant in the battle of Calatafimi, where the royal troops made their first stand, and which was the hardest fight of the campaign and the most brilliant of all Garibaldi's victories, defeating four times the number of his own army of disciplined troops under an able commander, posted in strong defensive positions, which had to be carried by direct assault, one after the other, and the last with a bayonet charge, the ammunition being nearly exhausted. Here Crispi distinguished himself in the combat, and, the fighting over and the army of General Lanza in retreat, he set to work to organise the ambulance service with the tireless activity which is the chief trait of the man. Finding one of the men, after an operation, shirtless, his shirt having been cut away by the surgeons, and the night being fresh, Crispi divested himself of his only undergarment, for extra clothing in the impedimenta of The Thousand was limited, and gave it to the wounded man. Years after, as he was walking in the streets of Leghorn, he was accosted by a stranger in words of affectionate reminder, but Crispi in vain tried to recall his face. He was the volunteer to whom he had given his shirt at Calatafimi. At Alcamo there was a beginning of organisation of government, and Crispi appears as the Secretary of State to the Dictator, appointing governors of provinces and providing for the nomination of officers of public security and civic councils. The years of Crispi's isolation and solitary reflection on the affairs of his Sicily had been largely spent in the study of the details of constitutional government, and the papers which puzzled the inquisitors of Turin when they searched his quarters,

expecting to find the details of plots for insurrection, and found only embryo constitutions
and projects of laws, were now to be applied
to practical organisation. At Partinico a
decree was issued authorising the communes
to compensate the population for the damages
caused by the royal troops, to be refunded to
the communes after the restoration of peace,
a measure which threw the interests of the
population on the side of the Revolution and
gave courage to the friends of it. Other
decrees constituted a council of war for the
army and promulgated the civil code of the
kingdom of Sardinia for the civilians, abolish-
ing as far as possible the Bourbon regime from
the beginning.

At Monreale the Neapolitan army, in strong
positions and in largely superior strength,
blocked the road to Palermo, and the chiefs
were divided in their opinions as to the course
to be taken. Most of them advised the direct
attack on the positions of Monreale, some the
withdrawal into the interior and making a
harassing campaign against the Government.
Crispi almost alone, knowing every foot of
the ground and the strength and difficulties
of the position, advised turning it and attacking
Palermo from the other side. Garibaldi yielded
to the considerations of his assistant chief of
staff, and leaving Rosolino Pilo and his bands
of Sicilians to keep up the appearance of an

attack from that side, and making a feint of moving his main body in the same direction, fell back, and by night commenced his march by the mountains round to the eastern side of the city. The troops followed, and, being deceived by a ruse of Garibaldi—the sending of his artillery with a small detachment by a mountain road into the interior—pursued that, while Garibaldi with the bulk of the force turned northward, and, marching all night, arrived before the eastern gates of Palermo before day. Crispi was at the head of one of the three columns which entered the city and met in the streets, where for four days the fighting went on, ending in the retreat of the troops to the fortress and, after a short delay, their embarkation for Naples. The Cabinet of the Dictator was composed of Crispi, with the portfolios of finance and the interior; Colonel Orsini, of war; Guarnieri, of justice, instruction, and worship; Ugdulena, of foreign affairs and commerce; Baron Casimir Pisani, of commerce. The first work of the new Government was to restore in the main the constitution and general condition of the island under the regime of 1849.

History has recorded the remarkable period of tranquillity and legality which prevailed in the island during the dictatorship of Garibaldi, an interregnum of order between the turbulence of the Bourbon rule and the deplorable state into which it fell in the later times, when the union with Italy was a *fait accompli*. It seemed as if the pride of the islanders was so thoroughly enlisted in the preservation of legality that even the ancient and traditional brigandage was suppressed by the universal pressure of the public opinion, not often in any part of Italy south of the Appenines enlisted on the part of the authorities, but in Sicily especially hostile to the ruling powers from time immemorial. Crispi was left as the Secretary of State to conduct the Government established at Palermo, while Garibaldi carried on the military operations in a march eastward, meeting at Milazzo a determined and for a moment successful resistance. His genius and tenacity triumphed, and the Neapolitan troops, driven into the fortress, took ship for Naples, and, except Messina, Sicily was liberated. One of the first measures of Crispi was for the distribution of the feudal and ecclesiastical domains amongst the men who took part in the Revolution, and another was for the adoption of the children of all who fell in the struggle. The temporary adoption of the Sardinian code subsequently gave place to one which was shaped by the needs of the population, and all the ruling agents were men who knew and sympathised with them ; and every Sicilian who hated the old regime felt himself a part of the new Government. This is not an isolated phenomenon in Italian and revolutionary epochs, and it may be that much of the orderly deportment of the islanders was simply due to the novelty of liberty and the pride in what they had done. The Government itself worked smoothly, and while Garibaldi organised the forces which gathered to him for the pursuit of his ulterior plans, Sicily was restored to order and tranquillity, the Bourbon authorities only holding some of the fortified places.

But the opposition which had failed to prevent the expedition, and the distrust which had followed it, soon began to work mischief. The plan of Garibaldi, in which Crispi had from the beginning supported him, was to make of Sicily a base for his operations against Naples, and then from Naples to work against the states of the Church, retaining each province under his own authority until the whole were free, when by a general movement Italy was to be united under the King of Sardinia as King of Italy. The plan of Cavour was, probably, rather to annex it part by part, as liberated, to Piedmont. Cavour evidently had apprehensions of the Republican propaganda ; he distrusted and even hated Mazzini and all Mazzinians, Crispi included, and the proclamation of " Italy and Vittorio Emanuele " with which the liberators opened the campaign, and carried it on to the last, did not allay his

antipathies.   They crop out in his correspondence ; to those who study events which are
complete in themselves and in their consequences, it is easy to criticise and show what
would have been better, as it is difficult to
assign to their proper source the responsibility
for mistakes which have happened.   Cavour
was apprehensive that the influence of Garibaldi might give place to that of Mazzini,
and that there might determine a Republican
tendency which it would be impossible to
combat, once the organisation of Sicily and
Naples had been even provisionally completed.
He did not know Crispi or he would have
understood that his influence could only be in
the direction of the unity of Italy, and would
never have been factiously employed.   But
the comprehensiveness of Garibaldi's plan of
operations probably inspired in Cavour an
apprehension that they meant disaster in the
long run.   He writes to the Countess de
Circourt (24th October 1860) : " Austria, it
seems, thinks of profiting by the absence of
the King and of our best divisions to attack us.
We are preparing to offer a desperate resistance.
If Cialdini and Fanti are at Naples [this was
during the campaign of Gaeta] we have here
La Marmora and Sonnaz, who are not fright-
ened at Benedek and the Archduke Albert."
With this feeling of new dangers to be apprehended from that side it was explicable that

he should view with the greatest anxiety an
ultimate attack on the states of the Church by
Garibaldi, and that he should be urgently
moved to get the control of the movement in
Sicily and in Naples at the earliest moment.
But with all this he chose his measures and
his men badly. He sent to the island a man
who he must have known could only disagree
with Crispi and probably with Garibaldi, La
Farina, who had at the outset done all he
could to make the plan of the expedition
abortive. He arrived on the 7th of June,
after the administration of the affairs of the
island was in a good way, on a Sardinian
frigate. Garibaldi had already conceived a
dislike of him through his having taken no
part in the new movement and from his want
of courage, for the Dictator could conceive no
man as worthy of respect who was not brave,
so that his reception was anything but warm.
Had Garibaldi sent him back to Turin he
would have saved much trouble. He remained,
in constant correspondence with Cavour, to
whom he represented Garibaldi as worn out
and in the hands of Crispi, who makes light
of his authority, etc., and after a few days
ventured to remonstrate to the Dictator on
the manner of government of his ministry, to
which Garibaldi replied that all went on
excellently well and "that Crispi and the
Government enjoyed the entire confidence of

Sicily." A Sicilian himself, the emissary of Cavour knew how to excite trouble in the city, and had his partisans, who were excited to make a street demonstration against Crispi and the ministry, which made Garibaldi furious, so that La Farina wrote to Cavour, in effect, that "the Dictator says that Crispi is a distinguished patriot ; that the expedition is due in great part to him, and that he will never send him away." Crispi's impatient and independent temper revolted at being made the subject of the attacks of the agent of the Government of the King, and he offered his resignation, which Garibaldi refused, but finally yielded to, on Crispi's insistence, on condition that he remained his private secretary ; whereupon La Farina writes to Cavour : "They say that Garibaldi has chosen Crispi for his private secretary : a grave difficulty for the new ministry, because the General is accustomed to issue his decrees without consulting the ministers. This morning the General, coming on horseback to the hotel to see Carini, who is seriously wounded, was accompanied by Crispi" ; and again, "Garibaldi leaves to Crispi, whom he has made his private secretary, all the real power." To show Crispi his good-will, Garibaldi appointed him Procureur-General to the High Court of Accounts, an honour which Crispi declined, saying, "You know, General, that we have not come to the island to gain high offices and good salaries. We came to help the brave population to break their chains and co-operate with them in constituting a free and united Italy, that Italy the idea of which has been the consolation of our exile." And at this time Crispi was a poor man, and for his services as Secretary of State in Sicily accepted no compensation. The result of La Farina's operations was that, finding Garibaldi inaccessible to his incitements to get rid of Crispi, he entered into an intrigue for the annexation of the island to Italy by royal decree, discovering which, Garibaldi expelled him from the island.

Carrying on to their completion his vast plans, Garibaldi had to appoint a Prodictator for Sicily, and had fixed on Depretis for the office, pending whose arrival he appointed Sirtori, with Crispi as Secretary of State. Depretis arrived on the 20th of July, and, accompanied by Crispi and Sirtori, went at once to Milazzo, where Garibaldi was halting after his great victory which completed the expulsion of the Bourbon forces from the open country. Depretis had come with the same purpose, and instructed by the same influence as those which sent La Farina, but, being a far shrewder man, he did not expose himself so quickly to detection. When he saw Garibaldi, he, however, attempted to urge the advantages of a speedy annexation, but received a peremptory repulse, which hardly left him a pretext to renew the subject. Depretis was a subtle, plausible, and able intriguant, versed in all the slippery devices of politics and the court, and he had come, called by Garibaldi, but sent by Cavour, with the deliberate intention of thwarting all the plans of the Dictator. Why Garibaldi should have chosen him was a mystery, but Depretis was a very Proteus of politics, without any principle and only the policy of getting ahead on his own account. He had the reputation amongst my colleagues in Rome of never by any chance telling the truth, but in my personal experience with him I found him at times perfectly frank, though it was clear enough that the frankness was such as suited the circumstances. Garibaldi took the precaution, however, to leave him with Crispi as Secretary of State, in spite of the latter's earnest request to be allowed to accompany the General in the remainder of the campaign, and Crispi yielded to the considerations urged on him. But he only accepted the position of Secretary of State for the Interior with the most complete statement of his conditions, chief of which was that Depretis should accept the policy laid down by Garibaldi without reserve, viz. that nothing should be done to precipitate annexation. He pointed out that during the execution of Garibaldi's complete scheme for the conquest of Naples, etc., Sicily was necessary as a base of operations, and that the annexation by throwing it under the Royal Government would at once stop his work and oblige him to return to his Caprera home. In case of a defeat in the Neapolitan campaign, he would be deprived of his necessary line of retreat and recruitment, and at the same time ran the risk of compromising Piedmont in his schemes. Besides those considerations, Sicily was not yet prepared for annexation to Italy, and required time to become so, and to become habituated to the exercise of its freedom and ready to pass under a regime of a totally different nature from that under which it has existed. This he knew was the judgment of Garibaldi, with which he perfectly agreed, and without a pledge from Depretis that he would undertake nothing to precipitate the annexation, he refused to accept any place with him. Depretis engaged to observe this condition, and they returned to Palermo to assume the government. And at this time Depretis had in his pocket a royal decree which, in view of the immediate annexation, named him royal commissioner, and from the day he arrived he did not cease to intrigue for the purpose of thwarting the intentions of the Dictator, and violating his promise to Crispi.

Such steps as could be taken for the
assimilation of Sicily to the rest of Italy,
without too precipitate changes, were accomplished. A Prodictatorial decree was issued
with the following considerations :—

Considering that by the vote given in the glorious
revolution of the 4th of April, with the unanimous
voice of the insurgents of Palermo, to which that
of all the other communes has responded, the Sicilians
have affirmed their will to be reunited to the constitutional and Italian kingdom of the august monarch
Vittorio Emanuele II. King of Italy :

Considering that the vote thus expressed is con-
formed to the national law, superior and eternal,
which leads the people forming one and the same
nation to unite ; and that the vote is consecrated by
the blood of those who, fighting under the order
of General Garibaldi, have carried in triumph and
crowned with new laurels the tri-coloured flag where
shines the cross of Savoy :

Considering that the other provinces and all
civilised nations have saluted with admiration the
programme " Italy and Vittorio Emanuele," and the
banner of the Sicilian revolution :

Considering that, if the extraordinary powers of
the dictature, which have no other purpose than to
consolidate the new order of things, tend towards
the ends which the revolution proposes, but do not
permit putting into immediate effect the fundamental
law of the Italian monarchy ; it is nevertheless
necessary to hasten its promulgation since that
fundamental law is the basis on which repose, and
are founded, the provisions of the new legislation,

all the jurisdictions and administrations of which have entered or must enter into force :

The Prodictator decrees that the constitutional statute of 4th March 1848, in force in the kingdom of Italy, is the fundamental law of Sicily, etc.

CHAPTER V

THIS decree, bearing the signature of Crispi at the head of the ministry of the Prodictator, was followed by others, which by degrees assimilated the legal status of Sicily to that of Piedmont. But this gradual approach to the union left too many opportunities for a miscarriage to suit Cavour, and Depretis, in conformity with his instructions and in violation of his promises, busied himself with intrigues for the fomentation of a precipitate annexation. Crispi, in the latter part of August, received a letter from a friend in Caltanisetta, which stated that Depretis was deceiving him and betraying the Dictator by urging an energetic propaganda for immediate annexation, enclosing a copy of a circular to that effect in the name of the Dictature. It urged that motives of high policy demanded it, and that it was the duty of patriots to urge it ; that the Piedmontese Government would not fail to recompense those who contributed to it, etc. Other copies of the circular from other parts of the island came to confirm the warning, and Crispi went to Depretis and, recalling the promises made and the conditions of his co-operation, asked him the meaning of these incitements. Depretis denied all; he had never had the intention to betray the confidence of the Dictator. "Read these letters then, since you so affirm, and these circulars. Both bear the mark of their origin, both come from the cabinet of the Prodictator. What mean these provocations, and what do your promises mean? Depretis continued to deny, to assert his ignorance of what was done, and asserted that the letters had been sent without his knowledge. "That is possible," said Crispi, "but you are responsible for what is done in your cabinet, and the most daring of your dependants would never have sent a circular of that sort without, I will not say, your order, but not without your consent. You know my ideas; you have accepted my conditions. What has passed frees me from the charge I had assumed at the desire of the Dictator and on your urging; I resume my liberty and only re-enter the Ministry of the Interior to prevent an interruption in the management of the business. But from this moment consider me as having resigned and look after my successor." Depretis begged him to reconsider his decision, but those who know Crispi will anticipate that he was immovable. A compromise with his dignity

or with an engagement, resignation to being
a victim of a trick, or a withdrawal from a
deliberate decision, are not in his nature. Much
less would he then accept an indignity for
the sake of remaining in any office. Crispi
waited several days for the appointment of
his successor, which never came. Depretis
feared the consequences of a rupture, and he
thought to wear out the indignation of Crispi
by delay. After a few days Crispi again went
to him to warn him that he had abandoned
the ministry, and that it had no longer a head.
Depretis urged, begged, conjured him with
tears in his eyes to recall his decision and
remain in the ministry. Crispi only replied,
"I have been deceived and may be again."
Depretis then asked what he meant to do.
Crispi replied that he should go to Naples at
once and inform Garibaldi of what was being
done. "I will go with you," said the Prodictator. "As you please." They went by
the same steamer. As Crispi had always the
entrée to Garibaldi's presence, he preceded
Depretis and had told his story before Depretis
was admitted, and the responsibility of the
intrigue to thwart the plans of Garibaldi was
discussed by the three; the facts were clear, and
the Prodictature was responsible. Several days
passed before Garibaldi came to a decision.
One day when the three were in the cabinet
of the General, Depretis came close to Crispi

and whispered, " I am going back to Palermo, will you come ? " Crispi only looked him in the eyes. At that moment a deputation of Sicilians was announced, and Garibaldi made a sign to them to withdraw, and ordered the deputation to be admitted. After an interval, Depretis was called in, and after a short interview came out and said to Crispi, " I have resigned." Garibaldi called Mordini, one of The Thousand, to succeed him and went over to the island himself to see what was the state of public feeling. There was no question that the island was with Crispi, and the new ministry was composed of men friendly to him.

But Crispi refused to return. It seems like an excessive *amour propre* which restrained him from yielding to the urgent solicitations of Garibaldi, who felt lost in the intricacies of Sicilian politics without him ; but those who know him will hardly consider that he acted merely from indignation at what had passed. His pride is excessive and his temper a fiery one, but he in all probability felt that the machinations of which Depretis was an instrument and he the object, would follow him whoever was Prodictator, and that in any case the tenacity of Turin would outwear the resistance of Garibaldi and whoever was in his place. If so, events proved that he was right. Mordini, who succeeded Depretis, was in honesty, patriotism, and independence of character, worthy the choice and the confidence of Garibaldi, but the network of intrigue was too close for any one but the Dictator himself to break. The refusal of Crispi was definite, and not even his attachment for Garibaldi could turn him. The Dictator insisted, employed all the considerations which the situation permitted, but to no effect. "No," said Crispi, "I ought not to accompany you. If I go, it will be me whom you place at the head of the Government of the island. That may be your intention, I suppose, and you will be so advised. But, they will say that I have imposed myself on you, and that you have imposed me on Sicily." "You are wrong," said the General, "we entered Palermo together on the 27th of May, in the midst of bullets and balls, and it is together that we will return." "They could understand my presence with you on the 27th of May; it explained itself. It will not be so to-day." Garibaldi finally grew angry and at last ordered Crispi to come, regardless of all his protests. He yielded, but contrived to miss the steamer which carried Garibaldi and remained in Naples.

On his return from Palermo, where he had installed Mordini, Garibaldi appointed two Secretaries of State, one for Naples and the Continent and the other for Sicily. Crispi filled the former post, but if he had believed

that the presence of Garibaldi, and his general
control of affairs would shelter him from the
attacks which he had to submit to in Palermo,
he was mistaken. The hostility which was
too shameful to be aimed at Garibaldi, was
aimed at all who were engaged in the work he
desired done. It mattered not who was there,
the object was to prevent the plan of the
General from being carried out. His own
popularity made it dangerous to make the
attack personal, but it was necessary to prevent
him from making Naples the new base for a
march on Rome and therefore to cripple him
indirectly. Bertani, one of the noblest and
most honest of the regenerators of Italy, who
was Garibaldi's secretary-general, *i.e.* chief of
the cabinet, was, equally with the others who
were faithful to Garibaldi, the object of the
calumnies of the Piedmontese party and finally,
weary of an official existence which only won
obloquy from those whom the liberators had
supposed to be the leaders in Italian liberation,
he resigned and resumed his place in parliament. Crispi was appointed his successor and
succeeded to all the hostility. The *Nazionale*,
the organ of the Moderates and conducted
by Bonghi, turned its worst fire on him : accused him, as La Farina had, of usurping the
authority of the Dictator, of opposing his
intentions ; called him " the evil genius of the
brave General, he who perverted the most

H

noble intentions of Garibaldi, he who troubles the public mind—he *was* Bertani, he calls himself *to-day* Crispi." To all this warfare Crispi made no reply. This has always been his habit, and with one formal exception,[1] until the attack in 1893 regarding the bank scandals, he has never, so far as I know, paid any attention even to the most libellous political attacks, a policy which had made the libelling safe and common.

The same system of petty hostilities which had made the position of Bertani untenable, was now directed against Crispi, and the Cavourian formula of attack was " No transaction with the Mazzinians ; no weakness towards the Garibaldians, but for their chief, extreme consideration." And this formula implied any kind of molestation for Crispi. At this juncture arrived Giorgio Pallavicini, a Lombard liberal, known for his prominence in the movement of 1821 and imprisonment in Spielburg, and whom Garibaldi had selected for the Prodictatorship of Naples. Pallavicini had received the instructions of Cavour before leaving Turin, and in pursuance of them he proposed an agreement between the Dictator and the Piedmontese Government. This included as one of its conditions, the

---

[1] He afterwards brought a libel suit with liberty of proof against the publisher of La Farina's letters against him, and gained his cause.

expulsion of Crispi, Bertani, and Mazzini from the kingdom. Garibaldi refused to accept these terms which seemed to him, as they were, humiliating and indeed degrading, as involving the repudiation of the men who had so powerfully aided him, and in Crispi's case, even guided him in his undertaking, and he declined the services of Pallavicini on the conditions sought to be imposed. Again Crispi, aided by Cattaneo, insisted on the appointment, the expulsions being ignored, and the decree was issued naming Pallavicini to that function on the 3rd of October, followed on the 5th by a Prodictatorial decree suppressing the secretaryship for Sicily and leaving Crispi the functions of secretary-general for the Prodictature, and secretary of foreign affairs. But the hostility against him was irrevocable, and decreed to reappear at every possible juncture. Cavour had no faith in any one who had ever been tainted with republican doctrine, and the malefic influence of the incompetent and treacherous La Farina had so taken possession of the mind of the statesman, that Crispi's constant self-effacement and devotion to the cause produced no effect, and were perhaps taken as evidences of his duplicity and the danger which his recognised abilities might expose the kingdom to if he were left in power. The curious phenomenon of the man who had played the chief part in

the only successful conspiracy ever carried out
by the Italians, and who, that the success
might not be a danger for that unity of Italy
which Cavour himself made the object of all
his activity, had consented to separate himself
from the political associates and sacrifice his
political convictions, should be pursued with
such malignity by the minister of the King
for whom he was so largely instrumental in
winning a new kingdom, is one of the most
extraordinary of the incidents of this unique
history.   It is at once a tribute to the importance of Crispi in the affairs of Italy, and an
evidence of the prescriptive and prejudiced
character of Cavour in all that had to do with
his dealing with his instruments.   He had no
insight into the South - Italian character—an
unflinching conspirator through diplomacy, he
had no confidence in revolutionary characters
or methods.   If he dared he would have
snuffed out Garibaldi as readily as Crispi—what
pleased him was entire subordination to his
own ideas.

It is difficult to understand the war which
has always been waged on Crispi from the
moment he entered the sphere of Italian politics
down to the present time.   It was begun by
the monarchists under the apprehension of
danger to the crown, and was later carried on by
the republicans under various and specious pre-
texts.   In the beginning he was persecuted and

imprisoned as a follower of Mazzini, and later denounced as a traitor to Mazzini. In fact he was never a Mazzinian pure and simple, but always regarded the question of form of government as a secondary one, while Mazzini held the Republic as the only finality. After having practically controlled the government of Sicily and Naples during all the time that the Dictature lasted, Crispi left his functions under Garibaldi in a state approaching destitution. The little remnant of his paternal estate which survived 1848 had long been spent and he had never accepted any pay for his services. If money could have made him conform, or office have tamed his Albanian independence, Cavour might have foregone the proscription which, surviving his government, kept Crispi out of the councils of Italy till 1878. The hostility to him was tenacious, unrelenting, and until the union of the Neapolitan provinces with the northern was completed, it was merciless. When Pallavicini had been installed as Prodictator, the dismissal of Crispi being waived as a condition not to be mentioned, the opposition to all measures which were attributed to him was continued. The plan of a constituent assembly, to which Garibaldi held strongly and in which he was supported by Crispi, was considered at Turin as a road to the Republic, and was violently opposed by Pallavicini, and the subtle policy of Cavour determined on bringing the matter to a direct vote of the people, and to the plebiscite by which the people of the southern provinces should declare their desire that Italy should become one and indivisible under Vittorio Emanuele and his descendants, as a constitutional monarchy, but Garibaldi would not forego the idea of an assembly, and the following project was drawn up by Crispi :—

Italy and Vittorio Emanuele.

The Dictator of Southern Italy, with the object of completing the dispositions of the decree of October 8th, which convokes the people for a plebiscitary vote—to verify the regularity of the relative acts and to decide the incorporation of Southern Italy in Italy united and indivisible, decrees :

Art. 1. An assembly of deputies of the continental provinces of Southern Italy is convoked for the 1st of November in the city of Naples ;

Art. 2. The deputies will be named by universal suffrage ;

Art. 3. The Prodictator of Naples will fix the number of deputies to be named, establish the electoral districts, and prepare the reunion of the assembly ;

Art. 4. The Prodictator and the ministers are charged with the execution of the present law.

The project was sent to Pallavicini with these words written in Garibaldi's own hand, " Here, it seems to me, is what we had agreed on. The project has my entire approbation.

If you are of the same opinion, send me a signed copy. I will sign it in turn." Pallavicini, suspicious of conventions and schemes of Crispi, saw there only a *constituante*, which was possibly the cloak for a republican pronunciamiento, and in a furious temper he started for Caserta, where the General was. Attacking Crispi in his anger, he was interrupted by Garibaldi, who insisted on his employing language in accordance with the position. " Crispi is the man who makes trouble ; if he does not leave, I will," said he. Crispi was silent. Garibaldi spoke, " Never will I sacrifice my friends to your antipathies, above all when they are friends whom I know to be men of courage and disinterestment like Crispi. It is him whom I have chosen, and not you." Pallavicini stammered, " I retire," and in his confusion, not finding the door, but seeing that some one offered his arm to assist him, he saw it to be Cattaneo, and offered him his hand. Cattaneo refused it, saying, " You do not know the real friends of Garibaldi, or how to respect them." Pallavicini sent in his resignation at once, and Garibaldi gave Crispi the charge of forming a new ministry, that which had served under Pallavicini going out with him. The Moderates at once began organising hostile demonstrations in Naples, and in the end Garibaldi, worn out by the annoyances of the constant and rancorous hostility to all his intentions and the men devoted to their development, and longing for his repose of Caprera, gave up the struggle, and left the field open to the opposition of His Majesty.

In transferring the authority assumed by him, and confirmed by the population of the southern provinces, to the " King of Italy " thus officially for the first time so recognised, the Dictator accompanied the abdication by the following letter, the last official composition of Crispi in his connection with the revolution :—

SIRE—When on landing in Sicily I assumed the Dictature, I did so in your name, and for you, noble prince, on whom rest all the hopes of the nation. I satisfied then a desire of my heart, and fulfilled a promise consecrated by numerous acts, by laying in your hands the power which by all rights belongs to you, now that the people of the southern provinces of Italy have solemnly pronounced in favour of your rule and that of your descendants in legitimate line.

I remit to you the supreme authority over ten millions of Italians, the prey until a few months ago of a stupid and ferocious despotism, and for whom a reforming government is henceforward necessary. This government they will have from you whom God has elected to found the Italian nation, and to render it free and prosperous at home, powerful and respected abroad.

You will find in these regions a people at once docile and intelligent, disposed to order as much as desirous of liberty, ready for the greatest sacrifices whenever they shall be demanded in the interests of the country and of a national government. During the six months that I have had the government of them I have only had to congratulate myself on the character and good-will of this people which I have had—in association with my co-workers—to give to Italy, from which our tyrants had separated them.

I say nothing of my government. Sicily, despite all the difficulties raised by people from abroad, has received civil and political institutions equal to those of Upper Italy, and enjoys an unexampled tranquillity. Here, on the continent, where the presence of the enemy still constitutes an obstacle, the people makes rapid progress (and all its acts bear testimony to this) towards the national unity. These results are due to the activity and intelligence of the two distinguished patriots to whom I have confided the administration of affairs.

Will your Majesty permit me a prayer, which will be the only one, in the moment in which I resign the power into your hands. I implore of you that your very high protection shall be accorded to those who have been my collaborators in this great work of the enfranchisement of Southern Italy, and that you will welcome to your army my companions in arms, who have so well deserved of you and of the fatherland.—I am, Sire, etc.

CASERTA, 29*th* October 1860.

The manner in which this prayer of Garibaldi was thrown to the winds is one of the ineffaceable stains on the career of Cavour and the Piedmontese Government of the time, and the result has fully justified the anxiety of Crispi to have the necessary time given for the adaptation of the people of the southern provinces to the new regime, so that the union might be the union of willing populations of different habits, laws, and associations, with only their aspirations and language in common, and not, what both Garibaldi and Crispi feared, the annexation of the southern stock to the kingdom of Sardinia, with all the inevitable violences of a sudden and unelastic change of relations, and the imposition of a practically foreign caste of rulers. The conduct of Cavour towards Crispi was especially brutal and unworthy the position the two men held in the history of Italy. Crispi had shown his disinterestedness by refusing all advancement in Sicily by accompanying Garibaldi to Naples as his assistant, when he might have taken the first position in his native island : by refusing all compensation for his services, and by withdrawing his personality in all the more or less partial conflicts in which the exceptional position and influence he had over Garibaldi involved him. He had shaped the generous but illogical impulses of Garibaldi to the situation at which affairs had arrived, always constant to the end in view from the beginning, union of Italy under Vittorio Emanuele, and if any man who had taken part in the expedition of The Thousand merited the confidence of the

King it was Crispi. When, then, he retired from practical politics after the departure of Garibaldi for Caprera, and went back to his home in Palermo he turned his back on all political advancement other than that which should come to him from the popular recognition. Mordini, in whom, till the complete assimilation should take place, the supreme power was vested, was a man of sterling independence, but so far as the formulas of politics went, was not in sympathy with Crispi ; but the latter was regarded as of too great influence to permit the clique, who in spite of the annexation still intrigued against Sicily, to leave him in peace. When, therefore, the voyage of the King, which was to mark the change from the old to the new order of things, was near, it was decided at Turin that La Farina should be made the Minister of the Interior to the new Viceroy, the Chevalier de Montezemolo, but the good sense of Mordini, remembering the past relations of La Farina and of Crispi, made this too evidently a menace to the harmony of the occasion, so that it was finally decided that they should only land in Sicily when the King embarked to leave it. Cavour wrote, " I do not like the expedient, which I regard however as admissible. But for the love of God make no more concessions to the Crispini and the Garibaldini." The war which had been carried on secretly in

Naples against the policy of Garibaldi when it was not safe to oppose him personally, and against his friends and the advisers who supported his ideas, was now to be carried on in Sicily openly, the Dictator being out of the field.

CHAPTER VI

LA FARINA, the new minister, and his colleague, Cordova, also Sicilian, made the Government so unpopular that the public expressions of discontent soon provoked a crisis, and La Farina, attributing, sincerely or not, the agitation which was menacing his government, to Crispi, determined to arrest him. During the night of the last day of December, the police sent for this purpose presented themselves at the door of his apartment and rang the bell. Crispi, living on the third floor in the humblest state, went to the door himself, and when the gens-d'arme replied to his " Who is there ? " by the announcement that they had come to arrest the advocate Crispi, he refused to open. They had no means of forcing the strong oak door, and concluded to guard it till the daylight permitted other tactics. As soon as daylight appeared, Crispi went out on his balcony, looking out on the main street of Palermo, and gave the alarm, " robbers, robbers," and as the people began to assemble he begged them to go for the national guard as there were robbers in the house. The crowd gathered at the main door of the house, and when there was an assemblage sufficient to secure the power-lessness of the police, Crispi addressed them from his elevation, denouncing the attempt of the Government to arrest him secretly and violate the liberties of the citizen. The agitation which La Farina had hoped to anticipate became the worst that he had apprehended, and the entire population poured out into the streets, while the national guard was called to arms. La Farina summoned the general in command of the garrison to order out the troops and disperse the mob, to which the officer replied by a decided refusal, saying that " It was strange that when the Government of Vittorio Emanuele had hardly become established it should attempt to shed the blood of the people." La Farina accepted the alternative, he resigned, and with his colleagues of the Viceregal ministry left Palermo the next night, embarking for the continent on a Sardinian man-of-war at Messina.

The elections for the first Italian Parliament were at hand, and Crispi was a candidate for Palermo. The same rancorous hostility at Turin, which had made his official relations with Garibaldi so painful, continued its work when there was no longer any question which could be materially influenced by the presence of any single individual in the new Chamber

of Deputies, unless he were indeed of the first
power and political importance, and this one
must consider Crispi to have been, in the estimation of Cavour, the most determined and
successful pressure being applied to prevent his
being elected.   Against him was nominated
the Marquis of Torrearsa, a well-known and
wealthy Sicilian patrician, who was elected,
thanks to all the pressure of the official world.
An influential and devoted friend of Crispi,
Baron Favara, with a prevision of this result,
had quietly and unknown to Crispi or the
Government, caused him to be nominated at
Castelvetrano, a little city in the south-west of
the island, where the family of Favara had
property and influence enough to control the
election, and Crispi was there elected.   And
here, at the first step of the legal political
career which crowned the efforts of his life,
the arch-Sicilian conspirator, to whom more
than to any other man the island owed its
entry into the life of Italy, the curious ebb
of fortune left him stranded.   He had not the
money to take him to Turin to assume the
place in the Chamber of Deputies.   His father
dying in 1857 had left his property in equal
parts to his two sons, deducting from Francesco's
what he had sent him during his exile, and the
remainder, the product of the sale of the land
that fell to him, had barely served his rigid
economies during the years of exile and official

existence with Garibaldi, and were utterly
exhausted when the establishment of order and
liberty left him a freeman in his freed native
land. A public subscription was made to
enable him to take his place in the Chamber
of Deputies. That the political life of the
Deputy from Castelvetrano should be marked
by outbursts of bitterness, and even occasional
savagery, need not surprise us. From 1848 he
had suffered exile and poverty for the liberty
and union of Italy ; almost alone, and certainly
with assistance from few others, he had carried
to success a conspiracy ending in a revolutionary
movement which assured the national unity ;
a republican of old and tenacious faith, he had
accepted the monarchy and the House of Savoy
as the safety of that unity and given his utmost
efforts to the annexation in principle which
abolished the kingdom of Sicily in which, independent, he might have been amongst the
chiefs of the state ; and he found himself pro-
scribed by the men whom he had laboured to
give the power they abused to his loss ; opposed
with a hostility they did not even show the
adherents of the fallen monarchies ; he had
risked life and liberty only to gain new and
more shameful persecutions, and it is not to be
wondered at that these results should make him
an implacable enemy of the party in power
and goad his naturally volcanic temperament
into those occasional demonstrations of the

worst side of his nature in the almost brutal, and to him more than to any other disastrous, attacks on every measure the Right proposed. Having made the great sacrifice of his nearest personal ambitions, accepted the compromise with his political principles for the sake of the unity of Italy, he was indisposed to submit to the perpetual insult which the conduct of the men in power constituted, and he showed his revolt as he had that against the Bourbons, by an irreconcilable hostility which was paid him back in kind. What made his position more exasperating was the fact that he had by his acceptation of the monarchy alienated the political associates of all his earlier life, and drawn on himself the bitter hostility of Mazzini and the Mazzinians, who could not forgive his abandonment of the Republic ; and this double hostility of old foes and old friends, the former not conciliated by the alienation of the latter, was intensified by the consciousness that the man was of a dangerous and invincible individuality. Cavour began by a fatal blunder and all the Right followed, they attempted to suppress the publicist as they had tried to crush the revolutionary, and they only succeeded in making of him a refractory and often embarrassing element in their politics.

Crispi took his seat with the extreme Left, where he has always remained when not in the ministry. He was a chronic opposer of all the ministries of the Right, and only during the term of Rattazzi showed a benevolence measured and considerate under the circumstances in which that minister was placed, earnestly desiring the complete emancipation of Italy, comprising Venice and Rome, but always apprehensive of the Emperor of the French, whose fiat in all things regarding Italy was then almost omnipotent. He took part in the formation of the patriotic associations which kept up the agitation for this emancipation, and was with Aurelio Saffi, Alberto Mario, and others in the council of the *Emancipatrice*, one of the most important of them. The representatives of these societies met in the end of 1861 to form a confederation of the societies, under the name of the Union of the Liberal, Democratic, Italian Associations, with the programme of " The plebiscite of 21st October 1860, Rome capital, political equality amongst all classes of Italians, the armed nation according to the idea of Garibaldi," with the office of advocating a strict supervision of the internal and external relations of Italy, preparation of the national defence, and the protection of the liberty of the press. A deputation of the committees of supervision, composed of Crispi, Mordini, Musolino, Miceli, and Dolfi, was sent to Caprera to communicate to Garibaldi what had been done and what it was determined to do. The General promised his aid, and presided at the first sitting of the committee, designating Crispi as his substitute for the subsequent meetings. The assembly concluded the proposition and active prosecution of the following measures of national policy— agitation for the armament of the nation ; multiplication of the associations for the liberation of Rome and Venice in all the country, and universal suffrage. This was in effect the programme of the party of action, for the moment in accord with the Government, and undoubtedly in agreement with Rattazzi and Ricasoli as to the ends to be attained. Ricasoli had given place to Rattazzi in the Government before any steps were taken to advance beyond the published programme above given towards the realisation of the remaining steps towards the national unity. Rattazzi was in secret accord with the committee, and it was agreed that the forward movement, under the lead of Garibaldi, should be made. It was arranged that the corps of Genoese Carabineers, under Menotti Garibaldi, should be organised with the destination, perhaps only nominal, of the service of the repression of brigandage in Southern Italy ; that the committee should be furnished with a million francs and a supply of arms, that Garibaldi should be sent, at the expense of the state, on a tour in Europe, presumably to prepare the public opinion in certain regions, and the connivance of the

Government in a movement on the Tyrol. In this assurance Garibaldi at the proper moment took charge, at the frontiers of the Trentine, of the organisation of the forces and material which the committee had concentrated there. Thus far the Government was silent, but then, with one of those mysterious retreats which have always been characteristic of Italian policy while the Government of France had any influence in Italy, it interfered to repress and imprison. On the 15th of May 1862 many arrests of the volunteers assembled at Palazzolo, Sarnico, and other points near the frontier were made, and at Brescia blood was shed. The movement was at an end. On the 3rd of June Crispi in the Chamber denounced the ministry and demanded that the Chamber constitute itself in secret committee, in which he would denounce, with the proofs of names and dates, the misconduct of the ministry. He was defeated by a majority of one in his demand for an inquiry. From that time he was the political opponent of Rattazzi, with all the volcanic vehemence of his nature. It was to this departure, and to this incident, probably, that the prolonged abstention of Crispi from all participation in Government and his chronic, and often unreasonably violent, course of opposition were due.

In the affair of Aspromonte, which followed closely, Garibaldi followed up in another field

the struggle for the national unity begun on
the Tyrolese frontier, and again met the mysterious interference from beyond the Alps.
On the reassembling of Parliament, Rattazzi
was violently attacked by the Left, and Crispi
took an important part in the debate which
ended in the resignation of the ministry,
which did not affront a vote which might
have had more important consequences than
its own overthrow.   In the session of 17th
November 1864 Crispi, with others of the Left,
made a furious attack on the famous Convention of September, by which Italy entered into
a compact with France to cause the authority
of the Pope over the Pontifical state to be respected, the opposition declaring this convention an infringement of the rights of the nation.
A division took place in the party, and the
convention was approved.   Mordini, the leader
of the dissident members of the Left, having
declared that if he had considered the convention a violation of the plebiscite, he would
have resigned and conducted his opposition in
another place, Crispi replied in a speech which
furnished one of his most important declara-
tions.   " I cannot," he said, " remain under the
accusation of a declaration which touches me
and my friends, and which would, if admitted,
put us in contradiction with my principles.
I am convinced that the national compact, based
on the plebiscite of 21st October 1860, is violated

by the convention of 15th September. I do
not from that draw the consequence that I
ought to leave the place which my electors
have assigned me, and where I shall remain as
long as I preserve their confidence. It is not
the first time that I have regarded the law as
violated by the Parliament ; it is not the first
time that others, in that belief, have invited
me to leave this seat. But a soldier does not
desert the post assigned him by the law, where
duty calls and keeps him, where he must, if
necessary, die under the blows inflicted even in
violation of the law. I have no other flag to
show ; mine is that which I opened when
landing with Garibaldi at Marsala, 'Italy one,
with Vittorio Emanuele.' Those who admit
another standard do not desire the unity of
Italy. I have said before, and have repeated
in the communes that I have lately visited in
Sicily, 'The Monarchy unites us ; the Republic
would divide us.' We unitarians are before all
monarchists, and we support the monarchy
better than the monarchists of earlier date."
The sensation produced by this speech was
such that the sitting of the Chamber was suspended. Amongst the most important consequences of this position so defiantly taken, and
which placed Crispi in antagonism with many
of his oldest associates, without in the least
reconciling to him his old opponents, was the
formal separation from Mazzini, who attacked

Crispi in a letter, amongst the most remarkable he has left, accusing him of deserting the political faith. Crispi replied in a letter equally characteristic, and which remains the unchanged expression of his political creed. As an example of his thought, and the style which grows naturally in him from it, it best deserves reproduction of all his writings. I give it in an appendix. It is now, as it was then, the summary of his convictions and his determinations, and where he had varied from the strict conformity to its indications, it has been on account of practical obstacles, which he preferred turning to combatting. I do not think that an impartial critic can read it without the conviction of Crispi's sterling sincerity, political honesty, and patriotism.

CHAPTER VII

THE general elections of 1865 placed the Left in the position of a party which might aspire to govern. What prevented it from taking power was probably what has always been the weakness of Italian politics, the aversion to discipline and the personal ambitions of men willing to sacrifice the solid future for the trivial present. Except during the period of combat, and between the men of combat, there has never been any coherence amongst Italian publicists, and personal ambition, where it has existed, has always dissolved the combinations which the motives of the day have created. In the case of 1865 there were other causes unfavourable to a healthy party organisation—the brooding war, the weakness of Rattazzi before the influence of France, and the capriciousness of the King ; above all, perhaps, the impossibility of a really Italian policy in view of the deference of the King for the ideas of Napoleon III. Crispi was elected one of the Vice-Presidents of the Chamber, with Depretis and De Luca, the ministry having elected, by a small majority, their candidate for the President. Crispi was now seen to be a force in the Chamber, and in the composition of the ministry reformed under Lamarmora, after a defeat on a financial question soon after the opening of the session, his co-operation was sought, in view of the necessity of a strong Government to carry on the war of 1866, as to which Crispi had taken strong ground ; but the negotiations failed, as did others later, in which Ricasoli took the chief rôle. The apparent reason for his refusal was the differences which manifested themselves in the financial discussions, in the course of which a law for the imposition of the income-tax, supported by Crispi, and recognised as a necessary democratic measure, was opposed by Ricasoli, and carried by a small majority, Rattazzi and Ricasoli voting in the minority.

In the conduct of the war Crispi opposed the deference to Napoleon, and insisted on the purely Italian direction of it. Perhaps a suspicion of the inevitable adoption of the French programme lay at the bottom of his disinclination to accept office ; it is certain that his aversion to the Emperor of the French was always one of the determining elements of his conclusions. He was a friend of France but not of the Emperor, and this distinction has never been absent from his ideas of the international relations. The extreme deference of the King for Napoleon III. was the real cause of the weakness of Italy, and in this Crispi had no part. The war, as we know, was a humiliation. Whether Lamarmora had, or not, any cognition of the ulterior plans of the Emperor it is impossible now to say, but the dictation of the general character of the campaign accepted by him left the position of Italy one of questionable international good faith and unquestionable disgrace. That the strategy imposed on Italy by him in opposition to that arranged with Prussia left Bismarck free to come to an arrangement with Austria, which he could not have adopted in the case of Italy's having followed the arranged programme, is undoubted, and that peace should have been concluded at a moment when Italy could only show for all her preparations the defeats of Custozza and Lissa and the arrested advance of Garibaldi in Trent, was simply and purely the consequence of the dictation of Napoleon III. is equally clear. In all this Crispi had no participation except a momentary visit to Garibaldi in the midst of the operations in the valley of the Adige. His opinion of the campaign is put on record. He said : " At Berlin they have not forgotten that if the war of 1866 had not the result generally foreseen it is because Italy failed in the accord established between the two powers. If the ministers of the day had done their duty, if the chief of our armies had played the part expected of him, we should not have engaged in an inefficient demonstration at Custozza; we should have gone to Vienna to treat with the Emperor of Austria." On another occasion he has given this feeling a more pointed expression in the following words : " We never loved Louis-Napoleon. But from that moment our hatred for him had no longer limits. And our esteem for Lamarmora ceased for ever when we knew that he—he, the General—had lent himself to such ignoble combinations. The campaign of 1866 was lost because they wished to lose it."

In the end of 1866 was founded the journal *La Riforma*, the organ of a group of the Left—Crispi, Bertani, Cairoli, De Boni, and Carcassi, with Tommaso - Crudeli of the moderate Liberals, and Alberto Mario, Republican without compromise. The programme announced in *La Riforma* was one of wide reforms, as its name implied. It put in the forefront of them universal suffrage, excluding the illiterate; the *scrutin de liste*; the payment of the Deputies, and the incompatibility of the function of Deputy with any public office; the ineligibility of all who held contracts with the state or had interests subventioned by the state; absolute religious liberty and separation of the state and the church; abolition of the conscription and the national guard, and the transformation of the standing army into a national militia ; abolition or simplification of the special committees for the different arms and the military departments ; more rigorous definition of ministerial responsibility ; simplification of the administration of justice ; abolition of the death-penalty ; extension of the right of bail ; freedom and obligation of primary instruction ; autonomy of the universities ; abolition of religious instruction from the schools ; decentralisation in the administration of affairs ; proportional and progressive income-tax ; abolition of monopolies in the customs, and general taxation, with general sale of all the ecclesiastical patrimony. On all these objects few of the founders of the journal were agreed, and each retained his personal responsibility for his personal programme ; but the paper became a more or less completely reorganised organ of the entire Left, and, as the founders fell away in death or division of policy, it remained finally the personal property of Crispi, a costly possession and one which has perhaps done him more harm than good in his political fortunes.[1]

[1] Journalism is always a losing business in Italy if conducted on principles of honesty and public interest alone, and it is said that the losses by *La Riforma* to Crispi alone have been upward of a million francs during its existence and until his acceptation of office in 1893, when he disclaimed any further interest in it or responsibility for what might appear in its columns. It was

The Ricasoli ministry fell on the adverse report of the committee on the ministerial project regarding the liberty of the church and the disposal of the ecclesiastical property, and was reconstructed with Depretis in the place of Scialoia in the Ministry of Finance, but finally offered its resignation, and as the King refused to accept it, Mordini made an interpellation on the subject of popular meetings in the Veneto on which the ministry was defeated and, after a prorogation, dissolved the Chamber but was defeated in the elections. The new Chamber was convoked for the 22nd of March 1867, but before it met, the King by the mediation of General Cialdini made overtures to Crispi to form a ministry or take the Interior in one presided over by Ricasoli. But there was no community of ideas between the two, and Crispi again declined. The ministry struggled on for a short time, but finally, and for Ricasoli definitely, fell in April. In a subsequent discussion Crispi was accused jocularly of being a devourer of ministries, and after the manner of the man who has no perception of humour, he replied seriously, " No, I have never been a

for a few years longer conducted by friends, but with no authoritative character so far as Crispi is concerned. Crispi's large income in later years from his legal business enabled him to support, in great part, this heavy expense ; but it is no secret that the larger part of it for some years went into the support of the journal, and when he assumed office in 1887 he had created debts mainly for it to the amount of 240,000 francs.

devourer of ministries; all the ministries which have existed since 1861 have been devoured by the majorities which should have supported them. If in the path I follow, which leads to liberty, I meet Signor Rattazzi, I should be content, at least I should not complain. There was a moment in 1860 when the Hon. Ricasoli desired to follow my road. I commit no in-discretion in saying that, according to him, the programme of the ministry of which we should have formed part would have surprised the world and marked a change in Italian policy, a change corresponding to the fact of Ricasoli and Crispi being associated. But we understood that our meeting was only temporary, and that our roads were not the same. Ricasoli com-posed a Cabinet which did not know how to avoid the disasters of Custozza and Lissa, and I remained a simple Deputy."

Crispi was now the actual and even potent chief of the Left, then a party uncorrupted by power, and united by the associations of combat and sacrifice for liberty. Had Crispi been more ambitious of place the party had then taken the Government, and had its members been as rigid in their conception of party dis-cipline as he was, the accession of the party was inevitable. But Depretis, who later became the creator of the invertebrate party organism known as " Transformism " had already begun the work which was finally to destroy all traces of party organisation and parliamentary discipline, and the Left was not united. Crispi held to its rigid maintenance of its principles, and in the subsequent discussions he defined them in their relation to the situation. " What are we ? We are they who believed that the achievement of unity should precede that of liberty, even at the price of the sacrifice of the latter. But to-day that the question of Venice is settled we who would have employed any means for the redemption of this Italian land, and the securing of our independence, we are of the opinion that it is necessary to change the system and have recourse to no other arm than liberty—liberty should give us what we still lack. My duty is then to proclaim here, in the midst of the representatives of the nation, that it is only in re-organising our interior administration, in consolidating our institutions, that we shall obtain what remains of Italian soil in the hands of the foreigner. This is the reason that we are opposed to any act of aggression against the other European powers. What do we wish ? We wish an internal administration as simple and economical as possible ; we wish taxes well arranged and less burthensome ; we wish, finally, a real liberty and not the seeming of liberty which we have thus far enjoyed. We wish that Italy should be consolidated as a nation, convinced that, once consolidated, the return to the mother-country of those regions of Italy which are still in the hands of the foreigner will be the natural compliment of what we have done, and, I will say, the reward of our wisdom. To-day liberty and civilisation are more potent than the cannon. If there be still some who think that because some of us have been at Marsala and Friuli, our party still dreams of renewing those rash attempts, they deceive themselves and strangely misunderstand our intentions. Everything has its day, and our party is not fossilised. In politics the conduct of men ought to change with time and the social and political condition of the country. What ought not to vary is the end we propose to ourselves."

The definite fall of Ricasoli and the acceptation of the office of forming the new ministry by Rattazzi, brought Crispi to the front again. Rattazzi offered him a post in the Cabinet. This time he declined on account of his relations with Garibaldi. The General was at this time contemplating the expedition which was to end at Mentana, and Crispi being in his confidence and unable to dissuade him from the undertaking, declined an offer which he foresaw might bring him into antagonism with the chief who held his devotion. He attempted to dissuade him from the attempt until there had been at least a rising in Rome, and predicted, what Garibaldi had refused to contemplate as possible, the intervention of the Emperor of France. The General was immovable, and Crispi refused the proffered portfolio. There exists a letter of Crispi, written on this occasion, to Garibaldi, which says : " If you attempt a *coup de main* on the Pontifical States, in less than three months the French are in Italy." Although Crispi had opposed the Convention of September which guaranteed the frontiers of the dominions of the Pope from all attacks from without, he held it the duty of the Government to maintain it when accepted, and for this reason he was tenacious in urging Garibaldi to respect it and wait for the Romans to remove the bar by a movement from within, since the convention made it inevitable that the Government should oppose him, if only to prevent the return of the French troops.

But in fact the convention had been evaded by the Emperor even before it had been defied by Garibaldi. According to it the French troops were to be all withdrawn and the Romans left to their loyalty and their own forces. The Antibes Legion, so called to hide the real nature of it, and induce the world to believe that it was a force of volunteers devoted to the Pope, was in reality composed of French soldiers, some, if not all, of whom were still in the term of active service, and were under orders from Paris. This fact increased greatly the ferment and paralysed to a certain extent

K

the efforts of the Government to maintain order. A committee of assistance was formed, of which Crispi was the life, and which attempted principally to organise the movement from Rome, meanwhile preparing the means to maintain the struggle once commenced. Up to the last Crispi persisted in dissuading Garibaldi from the invasion, assuring him that the Government would do all in its power to prevent it, to which Garibaldi replied that he preferred dying to living in the shameful condition Italy was still in, and that he would not be dissuaded ; and when Crispi again predicted that he would provoke a foreign intervention, the General said, " A war with the foreigner would be the regeneration of Italy—if France should interfere you would be with me," to which Crispi gave his promise. But to the last day he opposed the expedition and only ceased to urge his views when he saw that the country was with Garibaldi and that a more forcible opposition would only bring on a civil war.

With the history of Mentana, and the effects on the politics of Rome and Europe I have nothing to do. Crispi was sent by the committee to persuade the General to withdraw to the Italian territory, when the intervention of France had become a *fait accompli* and the Garibaldians had been defeated, though Garibaldi even then refused to believe that the French were in the battle, and proposed to reorganise his troops for a renewal of the battle on the next day. Convinced by Crispi of the reality of the French participation he resigned himself to the disaster and was returning to Florence when he was arrested by the Italian gens-d'arme and imprisoned. Crispi made a passionate protest against the disgraceful arrest and contested its legitimacy in the tribunal. In the interpellations which occupied the chamber in consequence, he took a part, and in one of his speeches he said what has been shown prophetic : " The expedition of 1849 killed the Republic—the expedition of 1867 will kill the Empire," and it was the fact, then publicly declared by Guerzoni, that " Mentana had killed Magenta," which made the combination proposed by Austria in 1870 in favour of France, unacceptable, and by compromising the relations of Italy with France and binding the latter to the fortunes of the Temporal power, made the alliance with Italy and Austria for the defence of France, impossible. Having no part or influence with the ministry, Crispi had no share in the official responsibility for the decisions taken by it, but he was the soul of the opposition to any participation, moral or actual, in the events which followed, from Mentana to the invasion of Germany by France, not from any hostility to the French nation, but because, like all the Italians of republican tendencies, he opposed the schemes and combinations of the Emperor, as he had in the beginning the alliance with him for the war of 1859. Crispi had seen from the higher point of view of exile, that the alliance with the ambitions and dreams of empire of the Napoleons promised no good for Italy and its unity, and time has only confirmed his prevision, common for the rest to the band of exiles who from English soil had repudiated the alliance of Napoleon as politically immoral and capable of doing nothing but harm to Italy. That the making of Italy was too rapid and easy, is a common remark now amongst Italians who are capable of estimating the real condition of the country. A longer struggle, a more thorough realisation of the value of unity and independence would have made the union more solid and not have opened so widely the door to extravagance and corruption. Cavour's haste to bring into the system of Piedmontese constitutionalism, nations utterly distinct in traditions of government and life, was the gravest blunder in the shaping of Italian unity. The conception of the needs of the case which Crispi and Garibaldi held to as long as it was possible in the case of Sicily, was far wiser, as was the hostility of those exiles who opposed the alliance with Napoleon wiser than the haste of Cavour. There was no danger that the process, healthily begun and continued from 1830 by a natural law, should not work out its healthy fulfilment, and with all his dynastic blindness and absolutist fear of popular liberty, Carlo Alberto, in his *Italia farà da se*, had a higher perception of the future of Italy than had Cavour and Vittorio Emanuele in their over-hasting. With the perception of these things constantly present, seeing his Sicily misunderstood as he had foreseen she would be if too unpreparedly brought into a practically foreign government, in which her public men had substantially no voice as to the measures to be adopted in the forced assimilation with Piedmont ; attacked as he was continually by the Right as a revolutionist and a foreigner, all the part he had taken in the accomplished union absolutely ignored by those in power, it is not strange that what happened should happen—that Crispi with his violent and impulsive temperament, should attack every compromise with his ideals of government, and be a perpetual irreconcilable in Parliament, as he became, and that in spite of his universally recognised abilities, and occasional overtures from the succesive Cabinet makers, he should steadily refuse to take part in any ministry which was not ready to accept his programme. Almost invariably in extreme opposition, and always in the front of it, even his political friends were not always with him in his advance, but he has never been afraid to stand alone, and almost as often constituted the forlorn hope as led it. As Italian politics are conducted this was not a nature to be in the ministry, and the inevitable, under the circumstances, happened. What might have happened in the other, and possible case, of his becoming the actual director of the opposition, as he was the moral leader, it is useless to conjecture, but it is certain that if the same rigidity of his ideals of government which prevented him from becoming a member of a ministry, had not also prevented him from accepting the compromises of a party, as parties are made up in Italy, and becoming the tactical head of it, he would have been prime minister long before he was so. If I know the man, there entered also into this conclusion the conviction that as minister he would be obliged to throw overboard all ideals which were too advanced to enrol a majority in their support, and he determined to wait till his programme was possible of execution. His hopes were destined to perpetual disappointment. Generations must elapse before the men who must, or will, govern Italy can be made to see that local interests and sectional claims must be disciplined to the general good, and that no advance is made when the principles of government are sacrificed to momentary or local advantages. In the effort to educate his party, Crispi attempted to shape the opposition to his conception of what the majority should be. That portion of the programme of reforms published in *La Riforma* which was his own, he reiterated in a publication on the occasion of the accession of the Left to power in 1876, but then he might momentarily have hoped for its actuation. While he was officially as well as practically in opposition he did not detach himself from his party, because perhaps he hoped that when the time came it might be ready for his programme. In the stage in which 1870 found him, he was still the almost solitary advance-sentinel of the Left. In the savage opposition which was provoked in 1869 against the Tobacco Monopoly, he was one of the most savage, and the attacks of party against party were intensified by the single combats of individual against individual in a manner which the later party history shows no example of until the futile and disgraceful campaign of the Radicals against Crispi in 1894-95. And in both epochs the main attack was always directed against Crispi. It is necessary to remember these things to understand how large a part of the history of Italy during the parliamentary period belonged to Crispi, as it had during the revolutionary period, and how completely his individuality was preserved through both. But unfortunately the concentration of his party for his defence was not equal to that of the Right for his destruction. Every art was employed to break him. Says Riccio, a friendly but independent historian of this epoch [*I Meridionali nella Camera*] : " His political action at this time was marked by great savagery. He followed his adversaries everywhere, in the Tribunals . . . in journalism with the combative, aggressive, violent tone of *La Riforma* ; in Parliament, where he demanded, insisted, on an inquest and finally obtained it in spite of the will of the Right and the Ministry, and the hesitations of his friends. Neither the immense wrath and the vituperation of his adversaries, nor their numerous menaces were able to move him, any more than the prayers of his friends and the defection of some of them, like Guerzoni. Sometimes he was left alone, often was followed unwillingly. A man of another temper would have been broken ; he pertinaciously continued the campaign against Civinini and his friends. There were moments in this struggle in which the Left was afraid of its chief, in which it wished to separate its responsibility from his. In the sitting of 4th June 1869 Guerzoni said that the responsibility of Crispi's proceeding rested on the whole party. On the Left many shouted ' No ! ' there were those of the party who feared to follow Crispi in the way he had taken. On the Right a thousand traps were set for him, and if he had been less careful, less firm and decided he would have been inevitably lost. He had few companions faithful and audacious as himself, Lobbia amongst them, but he had on the contrary many bitterly implacable adversaries. On this occasion there was published by Ausonio Franchi the correspondence of that most bitter and pitiless deceased enemy of Crispi, Giuseppe La Farina. There were in this correspondence the most incredible vituperations, tremendous accusations. They thus disinterred a dead body, and the passions and hatred of the deceased, vented in private letters, served as instruments to fight the living. Crispi brought a suit for libel against Franchi, giving entire liberty of proving the allegations.[1] The Court condemned the slanderer, and the condemnation was affirmed by the Court of Appeals."

[1] According to the Italian law of libel the defendant cannot adduce, in proof of his libel, the facts of the case without the consent of the plaintiff.

CHAPTER VIII

In the sitting of the Chamber of January 25, 1869, Crispi had occasion to declare his political programme, not in all respects that of the party proclaimed two years before, but probably those points of it which he considered of possible effectuation, and at the same time he disavowed the position of chief of the Left which the differences between the principal members of the party made impossible for any one. He said, in effect, "We are in a country in which the English customs are not yet possible. Be it Right or Left, no one can say that he has his leader, as in the House of Commons." But in defining the position of parties he said, "Between you and us there is a great difference; there are two or three reforms which you will never favour and which we have proclaimed and which we should have the courage to carry out if we had in the Chamber the means to pass them. ["Hear," on the Left, and on the Right, "What are they?"] What? Since you ask me to state them I will do so in few words.

We desire a modification of the electoral law, and you refuse it; ["Hear, hear!" on the Left and uproar on the Right] we desire the province to be independent of the political power, at the head of each province a magistrate elected by its citizens, and you refuse it; we wish a municipality master of itself with a syndic nominated by popular suffrage, and you refuse it; [uproar on the Right and cries, "Yes, and we will always refuse it"] and in regard to the system of taxation we are so divided in ideas and opinions that it is impossible to understand each other; [interruptions on the Right] we think that the State ought to have no other imposts than direct ones, [uproar on the Right] except the customs, which from necessity cannot be abolished since the question of frontier duties is like that of standing armies, which no state can abolish so long as the entire hemisphere does not abolish them—if Europe entire does not disarm. As to the octroi, your grist-tax comprised, from which you will not get even the expenses of collection, we would give them to the communes until other means were provided to support the municipal finances [contradictions at the Right]." In passing it may be said that in some of these respects Crispi is not now so positive as when this statement was made, and that his ideas of the practicable and the necessary compromises in

financial difficulties, as well as his experience
in a larger liberty than Italy had then enjoyed
have brought him nearer to the position of
the Right than he could then have believed
possible.   But Italy had not then been under
the influence of all the corrupting agencies to
which she has since been subjected ; parties
had principles and some responsibility if not
responsible chiefs, and popular liberty was
very restricted.   Crispi's errors were the
generous ones of a man who believed in the
virtue of the masses, and had not had the
opportunity to see that in certain parts of
the peninsula liberty and license had no ear-
marks to distinguish one from the other ; and
all of whose struggles thus far had been
against the usurpations of the ruling classes
and the merciless restrictions of the Bourbon :
and his experience in Italian politics had thus
led him to believe that there was a difference
in system only, but not in severity, between
him and the Piedmontese, in the treatment of
popular aspirations.

After the transference of the Capital to
Florence, Crispi's legal practice had increased
greatly and interfered with his functions as
Deputy ; he had built himself a house which
called for expenditure, which made attention
to his practice imperative, and his marital
relations were most unfortunate for a public
man, and both during his Florentine residence

and after the transfer of the Capital to Rome, he was strongly disposed to withdraw from public affairs, and in fact did send in his resignation as Deputy, withdrawing it only on an unanimous vote of the Chamber not to accept it. He felt that the acquisition of the national Capital, Rome, and the possibility of the political completion of Italy making the future smoother, left him free to follow his own interests. He had never been ambitious of office, and had refused it when it imposed on him conditions which were entangling. He found office impossible without alliances which were not to his taste, and when finally he consented as a citizen to a fusion of forces with other parties than that to which he had always been allied, and which he had in fact led to some of its most important if rare victories, he was attacked by the Radicals, and even by old friends, as having betrayed the Democracy. In a speech at a public meeting after the occupation of Rome he defended himself from that charge in a discourse which was a renewal of the old watchword of Marsala, "Unity under the House of Savoy." After having shown why the movements of 1848 failed, he said: "Then came the days of exile, of hopes and of delusions. We believed that the Democracy to which was owing the conception of Unity would have been able to attain it by its own forces. We made for ten

years audacious attempts without a real success.
In 1859 the people awoke again and displayed
a banner that was not ours. That banner was
accepted by Garibaldi, and he indicated it to
us as that in the shadow of which the nation
would be reconstituted. We yielded and en-
rolled ourselves under him. When, in 1860
we were to leave for Sicily, certain puritans of
our party wished the cross of Savoy to be
omitted from our flag. I replied that it was
necessary to follow the banner of Garibaldi,
and that it must be accepted by those who
fought under him. We started and under
that sympathetic banner we debarked at
Marsala and went to Calatafimi where we
conquered. Schiaffino was killed holding that
banner. We were at Palermo, we ran triumphant to Milazzo and Messina, we passed
the Faro, we entered Naples, we got as far as
the Volturno; and with that sympathetic
banner we have conquered Venice and have
arrived at Rome. Certainly we have not sacrificed our principles, but we had the virtue of
yielding, knowing that we could not obtain the
national unity without compromising certain
views, without accepting that programme
which, gathering together all minds, would
have constituted the nation. We are not men
to repent the accord which we have ourselves
provoked and accepted. We are loyal men,
we remain on the ground we have chosen, and

we remain faithful to the regime agreed to by all the nation. For us Vittorio Emanuele is the first citizen of Italy, the supreme magistrate of the national unity. We followed and will follow the accepted programme, and we will maintain it all our lives." [Interruptions, cries of " Yes, yes ! " expression of approbation. The speaker was compelled to stop until the emotion had abated. Shouts of " Long live Italy and Vittorio Emanuele."] " I have never been to the Pitti, as I have never been to the Quirinal, but I consider the King as the first citizen of the state, the recognised head of a great nation." [Repeated and loud applause with some attempts at disapprobation.] At the following municipal elections the unity of the factions was maintained and the clericals were defeated, but the accord was not long-lived, and the dissensions between the parties restored the clerical government of Rome for many years.

In the years following the occupation of Rome Crispi took little part in politics. That this was not due to any abatement of his patriotic resolution is certain, and I can but attribute it to a general discouragement, firstly at the grave discords in the Left, which destroyed its efficacy as a party and made him hopeless of the accomplishment of the reforms he considered necessary, and secondly, and perhaps more profoundly, at the persistent hostility, for it can hardly be otherwise stated, of the King towards him. And here it must be permitted to tell the truth concerning Vittorio Emanuele, and so far as Crispi is concerned I know that neither by him nor with his consent would it ever be said; but with all his courageous and unflinching patriotism, the King remained to the end a somewhat absolutist monarch; his prejudices never quite gave way to his constitutional obligations, and amongst those towards whom he had an unjust and irrational animosity the chief was Crispi. That the chief member of the Left, if not officially its chief, should not be called to form a ministry when the time had arrived to call the Left into power, was constitutionally incorrect. That Depretis, who had always been found pliant and subservient to the influences of Court, should have been chosen for this office, was not creditable to the King nor to the Parliament, but that, even in the case that Crispi was not ready to accept the office of forming a ministry, he should not have been paid the formal compliment of being invited, was a tactical mistake in the King. Crispi had from the beginning been most faithful to the Monarchy, had suffered the alienation of some of his most devoted political friends, including Mazzini, and had from the earliest movement for the Sicilian rising, been treated by the Piedmontese party as an enemy, and when it seemed necessary to conciliate the Left by some parliamentary concession Rattazzi or Depretis were the only members of it who could count on the favour of the Crown. Nor is the proffer, made under difficult circumstances, of a place in the ministry formed by an inflexible statesman like Ricasoli, whose chiefship was a full guarantee against Crispi's possible transgression of limits, any evidence of a different disposition. At Court they were afraid of Crispi. In what ways this was shown to him and what shadow of humiliation was thrown on him by it, we shall never know, for of these things Crispi never speaks ; but that it exercised a great influence on his parliamentary conduct could only be expected, and probably something of his later uncompromising and impolitic independence was due to this state of feeling at Court. The King did not like independent men, the Court was rancorously hostile to them and to all democratic tendencies, and Crispi was made to feel this in many ways which never came to the King's knowledge. Crispi was proud, too proud to attempt to conciliate the courtiers, and even to do more than he had done to prove to the King his fidelity ; he was not, and never has been, ambitious of office other than as a means of serving the country ; but his pride and self-respect were inflexible, and it is not impossible that he held his services to Italy at an estimation which was excessive and which prevented him from yielding precedence to men who had not rendered the nation a tithe of his services. As he had no official ambitions, therefore he never made a concession to office, and naturally in a country where the secret and unconstitutional influences of a Court circle were, and still are, potent in the direction of affairs, he remained in opposition, even when, as happened finally, a Deputy of his party became Prime Minister, because he had become so by concessions which Crispi could not consent to. If he was feared at Court for his democratic tendencies, he detested the Court for its interference with the progress of constitutional growth and its corrupting tendencies, its intrigues and its narrow regionalism. And between the two there has never been peace.

The conquest of Rome left Crispi therefore still less disposed to make concessions of his principles, as the need of agitation for the national rights was ended. He opposed vigorously the law of the Papal guarantees, by which the Pope was assured a practical *imperium in imperio* and exempted from the operation of Italian law, and here he has proved a true prophet, as in many other details of the national development, for the greatest obstacle to the completion of a national programme and the greatest internal danger to Italy is the Vatican and the vantage it holds

in the country. In the agitations which had
compelled a Government of the Right to go to
Rome on the first European opportunity, the
Left, and with it Crispi, had taken the leading
part and had indeed driven the ministry to
take that step, but the timidity of the Right
before the Vatican, and the influence of the
French party, carried the Government farther
even in the way of dangerous concessions than
the law of guarantees, for it proposed to make
the law one of international sanction. This
folly was fortunately avoided by the refusal of
some of the Powers, and especially England,
to accept the dangerous responsibility. But if
the national unity was secured, the national
liberties were still incomplete so long as the
constitution was in danger from the arbitrary
methods which had clung to the regime im-
ported from Piedmont. On one of the few
occasions in which Crispi took a part in his
old vein, which was in the discussion of the
financial provisions, he made use of an expression that no doubt retempered the old hostility
at Court, and which, if it did not exceed his
intention, did certainly exceed his justification,
and subsequent history has shown him to
have repudiated it. Alluding to the measures
he considered unconstitutional, he said : " We
are at Rome. Here you cannot and ought not
follow the abuses committed at Turin and
Florence ; either respect the constitution,

applying it loyally, or we will recommence the
work which we did against the princes dis-
possessed and sent away." (Sitting of 13th December 1871.) I have little doubt that had
Crispi at this juncture followed the urgings of
Mazzini and "descended into the street and
the barricades," he would have carried with
him the entire republican and radical elements,
the only ones which had any power of initiative
in the peninsula, and that a revolution might
have followed. But this could never have
been in the thought of Crispi, to whom the
Republic meant the division of Italy. In the
earlier phase of the movement he had avowed
that "unity before liberty" was his programme,
but when unity was complete that liberty must
follow, and he meant to intimate to the reactionary party then in power that the danger
to any form of absolutism was still in view and
that the nation would not be allowed to go
back. But even so the expression was one
which, while it is not possible to judge it in
full cognizance of cause and effect, was one of
those imprudences which Crispi's impetuous
and often uncontrollable nature at times
drove him into, and which his enemies have
always been quick to take advantage of. At
Mazzini's death he made the motion for the
condolence of the Chamber for the national
loss, and rendered an affectionate tribute to the
man who had been the inspirer of so much of

his early political conduct. To the memory of Mazzini he has always been faithful, ignoring the hostility of the master in those later days when Crispi had consented to sacrifice the Republic to the good of Italy. There is no longer any question that Mazzini clung to the Republic throughout, and though there were moments when he seemed willing to put the form of government in the background, they were only moments, and there is evidence that he favoured the French occupation of Rome rather than the conquest by the Kingdom, believing that it was the surer means to the Republic in the end. But Crispi, too, was intolerant, and the defection of the more undisciplinable members of the Left, in the formation of the party known as the " Young Left," found him inexorable in his hostility. In fact, all through this period of his life, while the boiling blood of his revolutionary days still ran unchecked through his veins, he was in the position of the master of a rebellious school, unable to exercise control over those whom, in the political order of things, he felt himself to be the natural chief over, and yet unable or unwilling to renounce the exercise of authority. This trait, which so much resembled personal arrogance, and was intolerance where intolerance was rebelled against always, made him seem dictatorial, but was in reality only a morbid and excessive sense of discipline, a trait which has always been dominant in Crispi's career in government and out of it : it was not a personal consideration but an insistence on the political discipline without which no constitutional government was to him possible. He is a born leader of the people, but not a demagogue, and this distinction has never been recognised except by those who knew him well. His passionate intolerance of insubordination will explain all that is attributed to a supposed dictatorial tendency, and which with his often uncontrollable temper, sent out flashes of despotism ; and as the prevalent and dominant political vice of the Italians is a chronic and all-pervading insubordination, Crispi's intolerance of it made him intolerable to them.

CHAPTER IX

But when, in spite of all the mistakes and vices of the Left, it at length came to power in 1876, it was Depretis who, for reasons I have shown, became Prime Minister. Crispi's position became that rather of a benevolent than an organic opposition ; but whether from his own attitude, or that of the King, he did not form part of the ministry was never known, and though by moral authority the chief of the Left, he was excluded from its first Government. One motive might have been of sufficient weight to make him refuse, even if the King had accepted him, and that was the participation of a secession from the Right in the victory of the Left. In this confusion of parties he was not at home, and as his contention had always been for the strict reorganisation of parties on the English model, which he never wearied of holding up as an example to the Italians, it is probable that this weighed in his decisions. At this juncture he published one of those notable discourses which always had the tone of a pro-

nunciamiento, and in which he speaks as if he
alone had the power and capacity of organising
the party—the tone which has always done so
much to strengthen the imputation of dictatorial which he enjoys. And he was only
wrong in this, that not even he was capable
of this reorganisation, for Italian politics, now
and ever, are incapable of organisation ; but
were it possible, he, and he alone, was ever
capable of effecting it. In this discourse he
enunciates one of the doctrines which he from
time to time put forward with the tone of
authority which perhaps he merited, but few
allowed him. In it he says : " Often the
authoritarians talk of the rights of the State.
This is an error. The State has, and can have,
no rights. It receives a delegation from the
people for the fulfilling of certain functions
which are attributed to it, and the people
which exceeds the limits of its delegation, and
abandons its rights to the State, is not worthy
of liberty, but establishes with its own hands
despotism and slavery." No doubt this, like
many of Crispi's formulas, was the outcome
of a perception of a momentary use of democratic rights, but time has shown him that in
some cases the people has had the necessity of
calling in a practical dictatorship, and he has
been the man who had to accept it. His
theories were too hard and absolute ; no
people, and especially not the Italian people,

has been so well educated in the practice of its privileges or its duties as to dispense with the occasional abdication of its theoretic rights. I think the later career of Crispi has made this clear to him, and, more than this, it has made him conscious that, as in Italy there can be at present no parties, so there can be no heads of party.

When the new Chamber met, Crispi was elected President of it by an immense majority. In this position, second only in the country to that of President of the Council of Ministers, Crispi performed his functions in a manner which is even now spoken of as exemplary. European affairs were then becoming complicated, and the position of Italy was in the balance. Crispi, during the vacation of Parliament, was charged with a mission to the capitals of Europe to ascertain the feeling of the various powers towards Italy and the probabilities of complication. Of this mission no official account has been given, and perhaps none can yet be given. There is only a letter written in reply to an article of Bonghi, an implacable and irrational critic of Crispi at all times until the last crisis (1894), which shows his work, but not his credentials. It is dated Naples, 7th September 1878. As an indication of Crispi's status at that time it is worth publication entire.

DEAR BONGHI—In the last number of the *Nuova Antologia* you published an excellent article with the title "Italian Diplomacy in the Oriental Crisis." In that article, discussing my voyage abroad last year, you uttered these words, "However that may be, as to the effects of that mission of Crispi, we can, and we ought, to declare that not only they were of no importance but rather injurious."

To express such a judgment it was necessary before all to know:

If I really had a mission;

In the affirmative, what it was;

How I fulfilled it.

Thus far the journals have written on this subject what was inexact or untrue. I have never been willing to engage in a discussion, and from September 1877 until to-day I have constantly kept silence from motives which you, a man in the Government, can understand better than any one.

At Paris, Berlin, London, and Vienna I took not a step without coming to an understanding with the representatives of the King, who had preannounced my arrival, and hastened to present me to the ministers of Foreign Affairs to whom they were accredited. With Prince Bismarck I had been for several years in relations, and with Count Andrassy, who was absent from Vienna, the interview was arranged by General Robilant himself.

You will certainly permit me not to reveal what was said then by me and by those illustrious personages with whom I was brought in contact; but I can assure you that Cav. Ressman, who was charged with the embassy in the absence of General Cialdini, Count di Launay, Marquis Menabrea, and Count Robilant were most contented with my conduct and with the reception I met with, and I had only to be satisfied with them.   There exist in the archives of the Consulta despatches and letters which attest what I affirm.

I shall not forget the spontaneous and frank exclamation of Count Robilant when we left the Cabinet of Baron Orczy : " You have spoken words of gold," ejaculated the valorous soldier, shaking my hand.   " You could not have spoken better, and there was need of it."   I will not repeat the words of Count di Launay, who was enthusiastic during my stay at Berlin, nor those of the Marquis Menabrea, with whom I was in perfect agreement.

At Paris I approached the republicans, and you are wrong in blaming me for it.   It was easy to comprehend that the unfortunate act of 16th May 1877 would be condemned in France, and that General MacMahon, after the manifestations of public opinion, would have the good sense to ex-tricate himself from the awkward position into which perfidious counsellors had drawn him.   It was neces-sary to make sure of the future ; and then, what shall I say to you?—my friendships in that country since twenty-two years have always been with the republicans, and I feel honoured by it.

I do not wish to judge the acts of the Hons. Melegari, Depretis, and Corti during the oriental crisis, and, as that does not concern me, I wash my hands of it.   I can, however, affirm that by my act excellent relations were maintained with the foreign governments.   After my journey the affairs of January and February last give important evidence of this, and the Green Book presented to the Chamber by Cairoli proves it.

Since April of this year the ministers of Austria-

Hungary and Great Britain earnestly requested to come to an understanding with the Italian Government on all the questions which should be the subjects of discussion in the congress of Berlin. They would not have shown such a desire if the relations between their countries and ours were not friendly, even cordial. Depretis could not respond, because after the 9th of March we were in a ministerial crisis, and Count Corti was indifferent because he did not know that it was understood that the agreements should be come to after, when, the military operations being finished, the moment for diplomatic action should arrive.

It would be useless for me here to express my ideas of the attitude which Italy ought to preserve in eastern questions. I will conclude my letter with the declaration that I desire to hasten the day in which the documents which refer to my journey of 1877 shall be published. I assure you that Italy was honoured, and I should be proud that my work with the various cabinets of Europe should be known.

And now, as a loyal opponent, permit me to shake hands.—Yours,   F. CRISPI.

The heterogeneous majority in the Chamber did not long maintain its confidence in the ministry, which resigned after a vote on a question of public security in which it had only a trifling majority, and Depretis called Crispi to his aid. He succeeded Nicotera in the Ministry of the Interior, and drew on himself, beside the old implacabilities of the Right, the rancour of Nicotera and his followers, who attributed to Crispi the exclusion of their chief.

He increased the animosity towards himself by the injudicious vigour with which he urged the presentation of the measures on which he had for years set his heart, and of which some were not yet ripened for adoption. He had not yet learned to make haste slowly, and now he became a goad in the sides of a majority, which did not care to move, even slowly. Measures which were no doubt of importance to the country, and which Crispi had long been ready for, the country considered to be interferences with vested privileges which seemed almost rights. One of these was the abolition of the Ministry of Agriculture and Commerce, by the Cabinet judged useless and rather a means to secure support for the ministry than a public good. The country had not come to the consciousness of the necessity of economy, and the Chamber resented the abolition of a place, the more that it was effected by Royal Decree in the vacation of Parliament. An extra-parliamentary crisis began to loom in view from the moment that Crispi assumed office. If Parliament had been in session the storm would have broken at once, but fortunately for Italy Crispi administered the Home Office in one of the most critical moments in its history, viz. the period in which the old Pope Pius IX. and the King, died. The delicate questions of precedent and formality called up by the first succession to the throne of the new kingdom were settled without friction, and Umberto became Umberto I. of Italy rather than the successor of the Humberts of Savoy of past centuries, thus satisfying theoretically the *amour propre* of the annexed provinces, whose dignity revolted at being made an appanage of Piedmont.   Republican demonstrations were prevented from taking occasion of the change in the personality of the Sovereign to question the rights of the successor of that King who had, by his courage and devotion to Italy, silenced reasonable discontent with the forms of a Government which could hardly have been bettered by a Republic, and asserting the national sovereignty against a young man without prestige ; and order was maintained by Crispi's firmness.   But Pius IX. left an embarrassment much greater than this behind him.   Crispi had in the Chamber opposed the law of guarantees, and the clericals urged the holding of the Conclave for the election of the successor, out of Italy, under the pretext that there could not be a free election at Rome.   In fact, the College of Cardinals had, at a first council, decided that the election should have taken place abroad, the legal consequence of which would have been the momentary evacuation of the Vatican, a situation possibly fraught with the gravest consequences for the Church and for Italy.   Only eight Cardinals voted for the holding of the Conclave at Rome. During the interval between this congregation and the second, the day after, Crispi, in a conversation with Cardinal Di Pietro, with whom he was on terms of ancient friendship, gave him distinctly to understand that if the Sacred College left the Vatican to consult, it might be assured of a safe-conduct and the fullest liberty wherever the Conclave should go, but that once out of the Vatican the Italian Government would take possession of it permanently. At the second congregation it was decided by thirty-two votes against five to hold the Conclave in Rome. Amongst the measures which Crispi, as Minister of the Interior, caused to be taken for the security against disorders was the prorogation of Parliament until the Conclave had finished its work, and affairs at the Vatican had assumed their normal condition. And even these, so great, services to the public tranquillity, added to the violence of the storm that was rising against Crispi. It was evident that at the convocation of the Chambers there would be a great majority against him, and at this moment came what seemed to be the *coup de grace* for his political existence, the scandal of his so-called divorce.

The precise history of this question I do not pretend to know—one who respected Crispi's feelings would hardly ask him for it, and one who did not would meet perhaps an unpleasant response—but the essential facts are these. When a prisoner in Turin, after the Lombard movement, he contracted a liaison with the girl who served the laundress of the prison, and when he was released and went into exile at Malta she followed him and became his mistress. Following his fortunes, she went with The Thousand to Sicily in the ambulance service, and during the following years lived in marital relations with him. As his fortunes rose the discrepancy between his position and hers gave rise to consequences such as might have been foreseen. In the *Life of Crispi*, by Felix Narjoux (Paris 1890), a book in which much is clearly fantastic and some things certainly incorrect, the history of the domestic disaster which this relation brought on Crispi is told with a precision which I am not able to say is incorrect,[1] but as I can find no better statement of it I prefer to leave the responsibility for it to the author of that work, premising that there is nothing in the account which is inconsistent with what we know of the matter, but much that is incontestable. Narjoux says :—

Rosalie Montmasson, become Madame Crispi, had naturally followed her husband from Palermo to

---

[1] It appears to be based on information given by Tamajo, a Maltese friend of Crispi, who seems to have been intimately connected with the history, having arranged the pretended marriage ceremony.

Turin and from Turin to Florence. After her experiences she was in honour. The survivors of The Thousand had made a subscription amongst themselves to offer Rosalie a diamond cross. She had received the decoration given to all the participators in the expedition of The Thousand, and a pension from the state recompensed her services. Presented to the King, she had been the object of a benevolent reception, she was surrounded by friends of her husband, accepted by all the men of the party of which he was the head. Garibaldi received at Florence the hospitality of his friend Crispi. Rosalie on this occasion saw around her all the official world. She had taken seriously the compliments and commonplaces which were poured on her, and drifted into an exaggeration of her importance. This new position, this unforeseen existence, for which she was so little prepared, took her by surprise. After so many evil days, so many vicissitudes, idleness helping, the mind of the poor woman became troubled ; she seemed to have been attacked by the mania of greatness. That was not all. Accustomed from infancy to live meanly, to count the least expense, she came, alas ! into disorder, not knowing how to refuse herself anything, wasted large sums in the most futile matters, in an exaggerated toilette, in keeping numerous animals, dogs, cats, white mice, canaries, etc., with which she filled her apartment. She called them all by strange names, and had for them the tenderness of a mother. Tamajo found his friend one day in a violent fit of anger : he showed him, in his drawing-room, scattered over the furniture, seven silk dresses of different shades of green, which the dressmaker had just brought, and on each dress some animal, dog or cat—one of the pets of Rosalie—had

M

taken its place. . . . Rosalie became little by little
an unsupportable companion. The friends of Crispi
say that he was never so unhappy as at this epoch.
His home, agitated, disturbed by continual quarrels,
had become unendurable. Jealousy came to take its
part. Crispi could go nowhere but his wife appeared
unexpectedly at his side, and the manner in which
she occupied herself was deplorable. (I omit here
what the author says of the fortunes of Crispi, wasted
by his partner and undermined by the diminution of
the value of his property, caused by the transfer of
the Capital to Rome, his legal clientele lost, and the
advent of a concurrence of disasters. These details
have nothing to do with the affair except to show
what Crispi had to endure.) Crispi was not the
man to allow himself to be beaten, but his existence
with Rosalie had become so odious that he expressed
his determination to resign from the Chamber, so
that no one could have the right to occupy himself
with his private life. He could, by devoting his
time to his affairs, re-establish order in his finances.
On the 13th of December 1871 he rose to speak in
the Chamber with the intention of never returning.
He spoke on the law of guarantees, and had an
immense success. . . . Returning home after this
memorable sitting, in which he had been so applauded,
he found Rosalie in a deplorable state. The pretty
washerwoman of the Palais Madame, become a fat
matron, was no longer merely eccentric, dirty, incapable of attending to the house or herself ; she had
for some time taken the habit of drink, and that day
she had passed all limits ; she was deplorably drunk.
Crispi fled ; he ran across the city, frantic, desperate,
and took refuge with Tamajo. What should he do?
What was he to become? He would not see this

woman again ; he would never go home ; he would
disappear, go away and never return.   He was ready
for anything ; he would undergo anything rather
than continue this unworthy existence, rather than
remain at the side of this creature who degraded him."

Tamajo, who had been the witness of a
ceremony which both Crispi and Rosalie took
for a real ecclesiastical marriage, but which he
knew to have been irregular and performed
by a wandering Jesuit priest who had no
licence in Malta to marry, and whose certifi-
cate was also signed with a forged signature,
now disclosed to Crispi that the marriage was
not valid even according to the law of the
Church which prevailed at Malta, and that no
legal tie bound him to Rosalie, and the same
friend took it on his charge to convince Rosalie
that such was the case, and that her own advantage and the position of Crispi depended
on the relation being dissolved, Crispi undertaking to assure her the means of life.   This
is the substance of the question which seemed
at the time to have wrecked Crispi's public
life.   As there is no divorce in Italy, and there
was no other way out of a life which had
become unendurable, the recognition of a real
nullity of the marriage would appear to one
who had no reason to find Crispi of an unprincipled nature, the wisest and simplest way
out of a great misfortune.   I think the justification of his conduct may be left to any im-

partial and generous mind, and to all such I
leave it, if any such can be found where he
is concerned, knowing Crispi's character as
well as any but a few of his oldest and
intimate friends can, and that there is in him
nothing ungenerous or dishonourable ; and
though his temper is a wild and often un-
governable one, and in circumstances of great
excitement capable of driving him to unjustifi-
able severity, I have abundant evidence that
he is incapable of doing deliberate injustice,
seeing it to be such.   I cannot blame him for
separating his fortunes from those of Rosalie.
And Crispi, like most public men in Italy, and
the East in general, had only the Eastern idea
of sexual morality.   To him woman was a
mere accessory to existence, for his life was so
absorbed by his political passions that they left
him practically indifferent to everything else.
The only person who, after his early romance,
has called out his real affection was his daughter,
to whom he has been ready to sacrifice his
life and everything in it.   To legitimise this
daughter he married civilly her mother.   This
act coming to the knowledge of Nicotera, who
could never forgive Crispi for having supplanted
him, as he supposed, in the ministry, was published as a bigamy, and the multitude of his
enemies, in Court and society, as well as in
Parliament, joined in an outcry, the fury and
brutality of which one must know something

of Italian politics to estimate. Crispi, accused in the opposition journals of bigamy, resigned his portfolio to be within the jurisdiction of the tribunals, and a criminal instruction was directed against him. The tribunal found that there was no evidence to support the charge of bigamy, and the affair was legally ended. But the effect aimed at by his enemies was attained, and Crispi was once more, and, if public opinion could be listened to, this time definitely, excluded from public affairs. In this affair the Court was, perhaps, the most violent and unscrupulous element amongst those hostile to Crispi, and even royalty was moved beyond serenity.

CHAPTER X

But the throwing overboard of Crispi, which Depretis effected somewhat brutally, and extending the exclusion even to the period following his acquittal, did not save the ministry, which fell shortly afterward. In the succeeding ministry Crispi was amongst the most violent of the opposition, and attacked Cairoli with all his early savagery, as he did the ministry Depretis-Cairoli which followed it, forgetting his early relations with Depretis in the resentment at his abandonment of him after the incident of the bigamous accusation. There appeared to be with the man certain crises or moments of volcanic energy in which nothing could be done in moderation, and the events of the crisis in his life just passed through had left the underfires very vivid. Under the violence of the attacks which Crispi and some others on the Left directed against the ministry, it was obliged, in order not to be defeated, to dissolve the Chamber. In the elections which followed, Depretis employed all the expedients which made his managements of the elections memorable and even proverbial, and Crispi was barely elected. He came back to the Chamber fuller than ever of fight, and the opening of the session was marked by a violence which compelled Farini, then President of the Chamber, to declare that the continuance of this tone of the debate would compel him to resign. But on the eve of the battle, perhaps from the habitual and, one may say, necessary reaction of Crispi's moods, he withdrew his interpellation, on which the debate was to be brought on, and shortly after resigned his seat, and though, after a vote of the Chamber which hardly left him a pretext to insist, under such flattering terms was it motived, he withdrew the resignation, he abandoned the sittings, and the ministry had a tranquil existence until the affair of the occupation of Tunis by the French. This event was the finishing blow to the career of Cairoli, who had been too simply credulous in the promises of France, and the ministry resigned without a vote. To the succeeding Cabinet, still always presided over by Depretis, now become indispensable, Crispi was friendly, and in the two following years he showed a large and statesmanlike disposition towards the higher interests of the nation. Perhaps at no other period had he exercised so large an influence on affairs, and the circumstances of his fall passed gradually away from the minds of the public. The Court alone remained always hostile, and I remember that one of the diplomatic body said to me just after this time, and when Crispi had returned to the ministry, that he asked the King if he thought Crispi a safe minister, to which the King replied, " It is better to have him with us than against us," a remark which of itself, while it shows that the common opinion that His Majesty has no personal or independent views in the conduct of affairs was mistaken, is enough to show his sagacity. Later years have probably strongly confirmed him in this good opinion.

In those years intervening between what was considered his definite retirement from office and his return, he advocated the reform of the suffrage and the electoral law, providing for the *scrutin de liste*. He gave up the struggle for the reconstitution of the Left, and under the influence of Depretis parties melted and recombined until the combinations of the Chamber were a phantasmagoria without clue or coherence. The outbreak of popular indignation at the occupation of Tunis, in which the voice of Crispi had been heard amongst the most indignant in protest, had caused him to be singled out in France as especially Gallophobe, and this was, so far as common observation goes, the beginning of the mistaken persuasion that he was inclined to a war

with France. Amongst the numerous misconceptions due to the very frank and often
undiplomatic way in which Crispi gave his
ideas to the world, the greatest was that of
his misogallism, and next that of his bellicose
tendency. Crispi never permitted the dignity
of the nation to be compromised while he was
responsible for it, nor did he ever, either then
or out of office, say a word or take a step not,
in his opinion, required by that dignity. The
difference between his manner of accepting
the slights and affronts which had become
habitual in the deportment of France towards
Italy, especially after the formation of the
Triple Alliance, and that of Depretis, who
always bent, and deprecated, and pocketed
affronts which he knew that Italy was not
prepared to resent actively, could only be
accounted for, under the French hypothesis,
by the desire to provoke a quarrel, while it
was in fact only the wise perception of the
fact that the only way to prevent provocation
from becoming unendurable was to meet it
far from home. The occupation of Tunis
could hardly fail in provoking the harshest
expressions of resentment against the French
violation of a formal pledge to the injury of
Italian interests, on the part of all Italians.
At this juncture, too, occurred the celebration
of the centenary of the Sicilian Vespers, and
the part that Crispi, chief amongst the children

of the island, took in the commemoration was considered by the morbid susceptibility of the French to be a confirmation of his desire to provoke hostility to France. It is hardly worth while to waste words on such futilities. Those who know Crispi's sentiments, and have known them through the years since this delusion arose, know that he never had a feeling of hostility towards France, and that in his large judgment the relations between Italy and *all* other nations call for peace at any other price than sacrifice of the consideration due her. But this disposition of France, or rather the pretence that this hostility was justified, had no small part in the official fortunes of Crispi. The men in the Government at Paris could be under no delusion on this subject, but the masses and the general political world came to a belief in Crispi's misogallism and belligerancy, which even extended to England.

With the conclusion of the Triple Alliance he had nothing to do, though he undoubtedly urged it after the occupation of Tunis, and his life-long, and in no case varied, attachment to England as the mother of political life and liberty, would in any case have thrown him on her side, should any difference between her and France call for action. He has never made a secret of his conviction that the way of Italy in all European affairs lay with that of England.

Although not in office when the invitation was given by England to occupy Egypt jointly with her, he exerted his utmost influence to induce his Government to accept the proposition. But popular feeling in Italy was not then so generally cordial towards England as it became later—the French had still a large party in the peninsula until the occupation of Tunis; and until the affair of Aigue-Mortes there was no popular hostility to France. The ministry of Depretis and Mancini in fact made a compact with France hostile to England, with the object of establishing a tripartite protectorate of Egypt in which the three powers should share, the object being distinctly averse to the occupation by England. Crispi's struggles against all this policy were probably the true motive of the French hostility to him. He was from the beginning opposed to the expedition to Massowah, and the speech in the Chamber in which he opposed the appropriation for it, was a prophecy of the disasters which have followed. This opposition to the colony in Africa only ceased when a military disaster involved the honour of the flag. The affair of Dogali, in which a battalion of Italian troops was annihilated, produced a shock in Italy which degenerated into panic. No one who was in the Chamber of Deputies in that memorable sitting when the Minister of War read the telegram which announced the destruction of the battalion, will forget the scene. It was as if they had heard of a new Lissa or Custozza, and the popular frenzy was on the same scale. The ministry was overwhelmed, and such was the violence of the Left against Robilant, who had only a few days before spoken of the Abyssinians as "four robbers," that the gallant soldier sent in an indignant resignation. There was from all sides a cry for Crispi, who had foreseen the disaster and opposed the expedition, and the old Sicilian again forgot his resentments and the Court suppressed for the day its animosities, and Crispi became again the soul of the Government. The death of Depretis, which followed a little later, left him as the unopposed and almost unquestioned successor to the Presidency of the Council. I do not dwell on the unimportant details of the parliamentary life of the period between Crispi's two ministries; the fickle public opinion, more fickle in Italy than anywhere else so far as I know, had changed from the wild execration and exultation at his fall, to the equally wild enthusiasm at the accession; the discouragement of the African disaster rapidly disappeared, and Crispi, no longer opposing the colonisation since the flag was in danger and the military honour of the country to be retrieved, pushed forward the measures for retrieval. It has been said that Crispi during his first tenure of the premiership became afflicted by a megalomania which involved a great increase of military expenditure and other precautions against imaginary dangers, or in preparation for prospective aggressions. There is not the slightest truth in either suggestion. He found the laws for the military expenditures approved when he took the office, and all that he did was to shorten the period in which they were to be made, and this was done under the pressure of the general apprehension of coming hostilities in which Italy was very likely to be engaged in fulfilment of obligations imposed by treaties which he found previously signed. He had simply to pay the bills of the extravagance of his predecessors and carry out the measures in whose shaping he had no part ; and in spite of this he effected economies in the administration of government to the amount of over 140 millions of francs a year, during the time he was in the control of affairs, and this control was uncontested by any considerable section of the Chamber. The hostility of France became acute, and sought opportunities to give trouble ; firstly in Massowah where the question of the capitulations was raised, not in behalf of French subjects, of whom there were none in the colony, but for Greeks, of whom France assumed the protection. Crispi, who held at this time the portfolio of Foreign Affairs as well as that of the Interior, peremptorily,

almost unceremoniously, repelled the preten-
sion of the French Government, and refused to
recognise the existence of the capitulations in
a colony which was in no relation with the
Sultan. The position he took was clear and
logical and there was no valid objection to it,
but his peremptory way of treating the question
increased the irritation of France against him.
His habit was to leave as little as possible to
his subordinates, and he was then excessive in
this disposition, and the occupation of the
Home Office tasked his powers to a degree
that left little strength for the Foreign Affairs,
and, overworked as he always was, his constitutional irritability was increased, and while
all the stories of his rudeness to the members
of the diplomatic body are absolutely false, as
from personal investigation I am in the position
to assert, it is true that his manners were not
what diplomatic customs have made *de rigeur*,
and exaggerated as they were sure to be, caused
him to be represented as insulting the Ambas-
sadors with whom he had differences to discuss,
and even those whose relations with Italy were
the most friendly were asserted to be the
subjects of his insolence. One story is told in
detail, of his receiving Lord Dufferin seated,
and of the Ambassador refusing to enter the
reception room till Crispi rose ! I hardly
think his Lordship will accuse me of indiscretion if I assert on his own authority that the

whole story is false, and that he said that he had never been treated with more consideration by any minister for Foreign Affairs than by Crispi. But there is no question that he always was plain and blunt in speech, or that he lacked the *suaviter in modo*, which so often makes the *fortiter in re* difficult to take exception to. For these reasons I consider his occupancy of that position a misfortune to him, though perhaps healthy to the country, which had suffered so much from the suave invertebracy of Mancini, and the unresisting duplicity of Depretis, that a change to the other extreme was perhaps necessary to restore the diplomatic self-respect of the country. That Crispi's manner to undiplomatic people was extremely unpleasant I had experience ; and to the press he was, if possible, more discourteous than to mere visitors, because he was at war with the press in general and neither asked favours from it or gave them to it, as a consequence of which the press war on him was very general. Before the expiration of his first premiership he learned, however, that it was his interest to be on friendly terms with at least one independent foreign journal, and he in the most ample and frank way made amends for past misconceptions.

The conduct of the French officials in many cases was provocatory and, especially in the case of the difficulty with the consul at

Florence, shortly after the Massowah difficulty, threatened to bring about a rupture of relations. That official on the death of a certain Tunisian subject at Florence, broke the seals which had been placed on his effects by the notary public of Italy, and possessed himself of the papers contained therein. As by the treaty with Tunis, all subjects of that government dying in Italy came, for the regulation of their affairs, under the Italian law, the invasion of the jurisdiction of Italy by the consul was a violation of law and treaty, and the Italian Government retook possession of the *res furtiva*. In the discussion which followed, the language of Crispi, while firm and inflexible in its insistence of the observation of the law, was unexceptionable in manner, and the French minister finished by admitting the error of his representative and the correct conduct of the Italian authorities, and promised to recall the consul, asking as a favour which Crispi readily granted, that the recall might be delayed until it could be effected apparently on some other ground, fearing an expression of irritation in the Chamber of Deputies at the concession to Italian dignity.[1] Had Crispi had the bellicose intentions so generally attributed to him, even in England, there was no want of opportunity

---

[1] I speak with certainty on this subject as I read the entire correspondence, which was, of course, never published.

to provoke difficulties, and it is now no secret that at one time during his administration of affairs the French Government was disposed to take advantage of the provocation it saw in the Triple Alliance to attack and disarm Italy ; and if he had been disposed to further such a policy there was an occasion to hand. The fact was that Italy was absolutely disarmed.   The guns which should have defended Spezzia were there, but the carriages were at Taranto, and the fortifications were so incomplete that a *coup de main* was perfectly practicable as the French well knew, and the famous project of a raid on Spezzia, the report of which sent the English fleet to Genoa, was probably the consequence of it.   The intention of such a movement was, as a matter of course, denied by France, for such things are only admitted when effected, but I am convinced that it was intended, and there is no question that the Italian Government received warning of it from at least two European capitals and on independent grounds.   The best argument in favour of it is that it was a bold and practicable plan for reducing the Triple Alliance to a Double one, for Italy was in no state to meet France on land or at sea, and I have no doubt, knowing the condition of the Italian defences in general at that time, that Italy would have been put *hors de combat* in three months, and obliged to sign any treaty the French dictated ;

N

while, according to the admissions to myself
of competent German military authorities, three
months at least would have been required to
break through the French frontier defences,
and by that time Italy would have no longer
been a combatant.   The whole plan of the
campaign was given in a book by a member
of the French staff, entitled *Rome et Berlin*,
published at the moment at which the *coup
de main* was to have taken place according to
the warnings given Crispi.   With Crispi's
knowledge of the real defencelessness of the
country, the responsibility of having any part
in provoking hostilities from which Italy
would have been the first to suffer, was one
which, with the most hostile predisposition,
he never would have accepted.   Of this there
is and can be no question, as everybody who
knows the man will understand.   His enemies
accuse him of a reckless audacity in his plans—
his history shows that his prevision of the
consequences of them was equal to their
audacity, and that they never passed the limits
of real prudence, and that while personally of
extreme recklessness, he has always been
cautious and safe in public matters.   A large
part of the intensification of the hostility of
France towards Crispi is doubtless due to his
intimate relations with Bismarck.   He made
two visits to the Chancellor, between whom
and Crispi the best understanding always

reigned.   There is no evidence that those visits resulted in any agreement as to definite points of international policy, but they undoubtedly strengthened Crispi's position in Europe. They may have been also at the bottom of the indifference of William II. towards Crispi, which manifested itself in later years, and probably influenced the attitude of the King of Italy towards his minister, for it is well known that the relations between Kaiser and King were of the most intimate and cordial.

CHAPTER XI

AMONGST the charges which afterwards made Crispi's fall acceptable to the fickle public which had so enthusiastically called him to the head of affairs, was that of extravagant expenditure in public affairs. I have shown that he really effected the first reforms in public expenditure by the economies in administration, and during his term of office he never proposed or levied a new tax, and, with the exception of a proposition for the construction of a new Palace for the Parliament, he proposed none of the great works which were supposed to be needed to make Rome worthy of her destiny as the new capital of Italy. The House of Parliament never passed beyond the stage of project, and the huge public buildings which contrast so strangely with the fortunes of Italy were the work of Sella. That Crispi was wise in this single proposition was shown by the necessity under which his successors found themselves, of entering into plans much more vast, and which, though yet unfinished, have called for

vastly more expenditure than the single scheme
of Crispi. His plan was to build a new
Parliament House and transfer the palace of
Montecitorio, a most inconvenient old building
for legislative purposes, to the Department of
Justice, for the use of the tribunals ; while
his successors, under the necessity of employing
the labourers whom the crisis in Rome had
thrown out of work, began the more costly
Palace of Justice still in construction, and the
great Hospital which, equally unconstructed,
will alone have required double the expenditure
he proposed. But Crispi's were evil days.
The great crisis which, in the last year of his
term, swept Rome and almost prostrated Italy,
owed him none of its disaster. Its seeds had
been planted in the banking laws from 1860,
and had ripened in the heat of the fictitious
prosperity of the great cities following the
removal of the capital to Rome. In 1887,
when Crispi assumed the direction of affairs,
the wild speculation due to the rapid apparent
growth of the capital had already begun, and
the financial demoralisation and corruption
had invaded the banks, over which, by the
defect of the banking laws, the Government
had no effective control and, by the corruption
in official circles, no efficient supervision. The
excessive and unhealthy demands of building speculation had exhausted the disposable
private capital, and the banks were called on

to disregard the provisions in reference to the securities for loans to contractors and speculators, and finally the ministry was called on, by an overwhelming public pressure, to waive the laws on limits and nature of the securities for loans ; and mortgages on real estate, which could not be legally accepted by the banks of circulation, were permitted in violation of the law.   The two men who controlled the financial policy of the Government, the most unsafe advisers the country has had for many years, Giolitti and Grimaldi, advised yielding to the pressure of public opinion, and Crispi, who generally accepted the responsibility of his colleagues in their respective provinces, for deliberative ministerial unity in the Italian system has hardly ever existed, yielded, and the last barriers to a safe finance were removed, with the inevitable result that the banks were involved in the ruin, only retarded for a time. Here Crispi made his first great mistake in government.   He should not have yielded, for his views, though not those of a practical financier, were sound on the banking question, and he must have seen the danger.   But Italy had been for thirty years governed for and by the banking interest, and its power was irresistible.   What the result would have been to him was clear to all disinterested persons at the time, since the Government that attempted to resist the pressure of the business

world would have been overthrown at once ;
but he would have fared better had he fallen
then and on the question of sound finance.

The period of the legislature was drawing to
an end—there was still a year to run, but part
of the Cabinet was eager for a dissolution, and
Crispi, though himself opposed to it, yielded
and went to the country on a programme of a
balance in the Budget, by economies alone,
promising no new taxes. There was practically no opposition to Crispi, and at least 400
out of the 508 Deputies were elected under
his colours, but he had exercised no control
over the official nominations, and all candidates
who presented themselves as ministerial were
accepted as friends.[1] In such a political
organisation, if it can be so called, as exists in
Italy, the only distinction in parties is that
between ministerial and anti-ministerial, and

---

[1] The invariable custom in Italy is for the Government to
indicate to the prefects, who represent the executive power,
which candidates it favours. This favour may be shown either
by active opposition at the polls ; by erasing from the lists of
voters those known to be hostile, both expedients employed by
Nicotera, Giolitti, and Rudini in the elections they controlled ;
or the indication to the constituency of the names of the candidates which the Government favours, as practised in all the
elections even by the most honest governments, this being
sufficient to determine many voters. Amongst the candidates
who flew the colours of Crispi at this election were Rudini and
others who led the revolt against him. Bonghi, Crispi's most
malignant enemy, begged Crispi, by personal application, not to
oppose his election, recognising his defeat as certain in the contrary case, and Crispi ordered the prefect not to allow any
pressure against Bonghi.

the office of the prefects, representing the
Government in the colleges, is to notify the
electors whom the Government favours. Where
official pressure is possible it is clear that the
result of the elections may be more or less
determined by it, but Crispi has always opposed
the application of official influence, except in
the case of men whose tendency was revolutionary—the ultra-Radicals, political Socialists,
and men who were openly advocates of a
change in the institutions. In this election
Crispi had a superfluity of adherents and had
no need of intervention, if he had been disposed
to apply it. The accusations which were and
are a matter of course in such cases, that Crispi
violated the freedom of the elections by official
pressure, are absurd, because in fact the majority
assured from the first was larger than it was
possible to discipline or that was desirable.
The Cabinet during the term of the legislature concluded had been substantially that
of Depretis, only slightly modified by Crispi,
and the programme was indetermined and
perhaps uncertain ; the elections were expected
to modify the former and define the latter.
So far as the programme was concerned, the
essential point was financial, and consisted in
the promise to bring expenditure down to
income by economies alone, avoiding increase
of taxation ; but behind these general objects
Crispi had decided on defined reforms, of which

the chief were the reorganisation of the currency and the consolidation of the banks of issue, of which there were six, the *Banca Nazionale*, *Banca Romana*, two Tuscan banks, together with the *Banco di Napoli* and *Banco di Sicilia*, institutions which are of anomalous character, their capital consisting of the agglomeration of the profits of operations performed with a capital given to them in the first instance by the Kings of Naples, and which were in fact government institutions, having neither shareholders to consult nor personal interests to satisfy. As assimilation between these and share-holding banks, which the other four were, was impossible, the plans of reorganisation were limited to those in Rome and Tuscany, and of these the latter, always well conducted and in the main perfectly solvent, offered no obstacle against the reorganisation in the abstract, the *Banca Nazionale* being the destined nucleus of the future *Banca d'Italia*, was interested in the transformation, and the only one of the six which opposed the plan of Crispi was the *Banca Romana*, mainly for reasons which subsequent events explained. Its Governor, Tanlongo, opposed with all his influences, secret and open, the proposed reform, but as the privilege of issue accorded by the law was to end in the following year, and Crispi had expressed the determination of not renewing it for the minor banks, the only hope of Tanlongo of deferring the disaster he foresaw on the winding up of the bank lay in the overthrow of Crispi. In the political revulsion which was to follow, and which seemed so inexplicable to those who did not know the inner workings of Italian politics when it occurred, the initiative of opposition to the new ministry was taken by the Governor of the *Banca Romana*, whose vast operations with political personages, outside of or contrary to the law of its organisation, had created a network of interests, secret but potent, which were practically at the command of the bank. With it, and under the auspices of the Deputies who were under its influence or in its pay, began the conspiracy which was to overthrow the ministry supported by the largest popular majority ever known in the history of the Italian Parliament. There had been a prior study of a combination between Nicotera and the heads of the old Right, in the October prior to the elections, but they did not bear fruit, and the Right for a great part, including Rudini, entered the electoral campaign as nominal supportors of Crispi, and the leading men of the Right were largely elected with the support of, and as adherents to, the ministry.

Early in the session the group of the Right which had been represented in the negotiations with Nicotera, reopened those with Crispi, and demanded the modification of the Cabinet and the admission of two of their number. Crispi said that it was not in his power to dismiss a minister, and that it depended on the King or on a vote of the Chamber against one, to determine his removal. To assume such a responsibility on his own initiative would be unconstitutional. This reply broke off the negotiations and those with Nicotera were renewed, the bank party giving the required probability of a hostile majority whenever an occasion should arise. The Vatican entered into the combination, backed by all the secret influence of the French Government, and though nominally foreign to the internal politics of Italy, the assurance was given that in the case of Crispi's overthrow and a consequent necessity for the appeal to the country in new elections, the Catholics would be directed to vote for the new ministry. Even the leaders of the combination did not hope for the continued adherence of a majority of a Chamber to their plans, and calculated only for a vote against the ministry taken by surprise, and that the combination would not stand more than three months. One of the Rudini ministry, in a conversation I had with him shortly after its formation, said to me that he was personally indisposed to enter it, and only did so in the firm conviction that it would not last more than three months.

The occasion for the intended attack was taken on the vote for a *catenaccio*, or decree for the immediate imposing of a Customs-impost contemporary to the presentation of the law to the Chamber, as a precaution against the anticipatory importation of the articles menaced, in order to avoid the tax, and prevent speculation. But there was not, under the circumstances, the ground for a hostile vote of the Chamber. The country was satisfied with Crispi's administration of affairs—his popularity was at the highest, and a deliberate vote would have strengthened his position. The secret animosities dared not openly throw off the mask, and only a surprise was practicable. The conspiracy was therefore carried as far as secrecy permitted, and it was then planned to arrange a combination to throw Crispi off his guard, make him lose his temper and commit some indiscretion, and then to rush a vote when the ministry should be entirely unprepared and the Chamber easily carried along by a panic. Bonghi, whose speech was of all the members of the Right the most caustic, opened the play with a savage attack on the old Left, which he accused of extravagance, etc. Crispi, in reply on the next sitting, retorted the charges on the Right and showed that the situation which it had brought about in 1866 had left the State helpless, with a fleet that met defeat and an army that went to Custozza.

The allusions were impolitic, and the heat was intempestuous in a time when conciliation as between the old parties was desirable and the finances demanded the union of all who valued the interests of the country more than those of party, but Crispi when provoked never was politic, and the attack of Bonghi, one of his oldest and bitterest enemies, was purposely venomous and irritating. Crispi fell into the trap, and when his reply was made, the violence of it offended some and dismayed others, while the confederates continued the irritation by jeers and contemptuous cries. The Chamber was stirred to a feverish excitement, and in this state of general irritation or assumed indignation the vote was taken and the ministry was defeated. The King did not support Crispi, the new ministers said even that he expressed himself as in the position of the young Emperor of Germany with Bismarck, glad to be relieved of the domination of the minister. This the King in later days distinctly denied to me, and I do not think that it is probable under the circumstances, but it was not then denied and had its effect in the forming of a new majority. That His Majesty had, however, practically abandoned Crispi is clear. That night a prelate who was friendly to Crispi, and who was one of my personal intimates, came to me with the information of the negotiations with the Vatican for the

support of the Catholic vote, which I communicated to Crispi.   He was incredulous,
but referring to his own authoritative sources
of information in the Vatican he found it
confirmed, and then for the first time
understood the importance and extent of the
combination which he had supposed to be
fortuitous.   Knowing the weakness of the
proposed ministerial combination, I did not
believe Crispi's retirement could endure long
and I publicly expressed that opinion.   The
next day I received a note from an informant
well versed in the transactions of the Roman
financial world to this effect :—" You are
wrong about Crispi's ever returning to power;
there is a financial combination which will
effectually prevent it."

Under the circumstances the King made a
mistake, it seems to me, in accepting Crispi's
resignation, the most serious mistake the
House of Savoy has made since Italy was
united.   The voice of the country was so
strongly in favour of the minister that had he
been enabled to consult it again he would
have been in a still stronger manner supported,
and the incident on which the vote was taken
was too trivial and personal to be weighed in
relation with the grave importance of the
crisis, while the calling of a ministry, most of
the members of which were without authority
or experience, to the direction of affairs, was

an experiment which promised disaster, and
fulfilled exorbitantly its promises. The banking interest resumed its direction of affairs,
and until the fall of the *Banca Romana* its
authority was not contested. For Crispi,
personally, it was a fortunate event that he
was thrown out of power at that time. He
was worn out with the fatigue of the double
office he occupied, and not only his health,
but his pecuniary affairs, needed his retirement.
His temper had grown morbid and dangerous
to himself and those around him. I remember
that in the latter days of his office, I had been
called to the Consulta to receive some ex-
planations on diplomatic affairs, and as the
interview was of some length, and the subordinates rather nervous when in attendance,
the one who had accompanied me to the door
of the minister's cabinet was waiting at it for
my appearance, and I shall not forget the
anxiety with which he asked me what temper
Crispi was in. His secretaries approached
him with apprehension. His domestic affairs
were at low ebb, for his ordinary income from
his legal practice, which left little margin
when out of office, was four times his official
salary ; and Crispi did not follow the practice
of keeping his office open with a substitute,
as mostly the ministers do, but closed it entirely, and gave his whole mind to his ministerial duties. A letter is extant from his wife,

written in the latter period of his first ministry, in which she complains that office was eating them up, and praying the Madonna to relieve them of it. To be free to accept office under Depretis in 1887 he had consolidated his debts in the sum of 240,000 lire (£9600), under the express condition that he should not be required to pay it till he retired from office, and when that event took place they had not been diminished by a pound.

The day after he left the Presidency of the Council the business world received his circular, *Francesco Crispi, Avvocato*, and during the three following years he devoted himself entirely to his business interests. He appeared in the Chamber occasionally and voted on the important laws, but took no part in the reorganisation of the opposition. He spoke against the Parliamentary Commission to examine the state of the banks, which led to the *Banca Romana* crash, not, as the report of the Commission showed conclusively, because he had any personal or corrupt interests involved, but because he saw, as did most others who had no interest or passion in the matter, that the promoters of the step were those who cared more for the weakening of the monarchy or their personal interests than for the purity of Italian politics, and hoped more from scandal than from reform. Crispi opposed it as likely to produce a scandal which would discredit the country, and proposed in preference the legal reform of the system of banking, and the subsequent unsensational rectification of the condition of the banks. He was right, for though the investigation developed the rottenness of the *Banca Romana*, it did not implicate many public men, and though it was aimed especially against Crispi, and the ministry of the day (Giolitti's) did all that was in its power to obtain evidence against him, the Commission reported that nothing had been discovered to implicate him, either morally or politically. The history of the country during those three years has little of Crispi in it. The weakness of the invertebrate government of Rudini, possibly honest, but timid and inexperienced, shrinking from every hostile vote and withdrawing every compromising measure, retreating step by step to the abyss into which it fell when retreat could go no further, was followed by the more crafty and far less respectable administration of Giolitti, living by makeshifts and momentary expedients, most disastrous in their ultimate effect on the order and finance of the country, and which, with an unexampled corruption of the elections, showed an unprecedented indifference, on one side to the maintenance of authority, and on the other to the solidity of the financial situation. The extreme Radicals, who had united with Rudini, the Right, and

o

the Clericals to overthrow Crispi, and then
with Giolitti to upset Rudini, were now pro-
tecting and stimulating a vast scheme of an
insurrectionary tendency, the ultimate scope
of which was the Federal Republic.   Before
this danger the ministry was absolutely im-
potent, both on account of its want of executive
vigour and decision, and its moral position,
impeached by the exposures of its complicity
in the bank scandals, in consequence of which
it resigned without a vote, on the report of
the Commission appointed to investigate them.
An active and widespread insurrection had
broken out in Sicily, and in the district of
Lunigiana, where the quarrymen of the great
marble regions had long been disposed to
socialism ; and preparations for a rising were
proceeding in the strong and always insub-
ordinate population of the Romagna ; the
funds were falling and the foreign exchange
rising rapidly, as the disorder spread with no
apparent possibility of checking it ; a great
disaster seemed imminent.   None of the proposed heads of Government succeeded in
forming a ministry, and all were obliged in
turn to decline the charge.   Crispi was, as
usual, opposed by all the Court influences,
and the King hesitated to call him until the
popular cry for him became irresistible, and
it was evident to the nation that no other
name had the power to enlist the public

confidence. After a fortnight of disastrous hesitation, in which the stability of the Monarchy seemed in danger, the King decided to charge Crispi with the formation of a government.

Not long after Crispi's fall in 1891, and while the ministry of Rudini seemed still in an unstable condition (which, indeed it never left), I asked Crispi if he would accept the government again. He replied, " Only on my own programme." In the situation of affairs in which he received the new call, there was no question of a definite programme or a combination of parties—the whole country was with him, the politicians were not. Of all the men who by their position in the councils of the country were evident candidates for the leading place, only one, Saracco, was ready to accept a share of the responsibility with Crispi, and the situation could only be met by the combination of all the moral resources of the nation. Never to any Italian was the Tarpeian rock so near to the Capitol ; if he accepted the post offered him *in extremis* and the ministry failed, the rapid overthrow of the Monarchy was inevitable ; financial failure was only six months away and new taxes must be laid on ; the insurrection was spreading, and in a fortnight would have involved the Romagna ; the general rising had been fixed vaguely for the spring-time, but in Sicily the spring-time found winter still in the Romagna, and so the unanimity so necessary in insurrection failed, and not the Government. Crispi accepted the charge, waiving his old resolution never to accept unless with his own men and his own measures ; it was necessary to save the Government and the Monarchy.

The formation of this ministry had a peculiarly dramatic character ; the rival ambitions stood around, eagerly expecting the failure of Crispi, though none of them had been able to form an acceptable list of ministers, and public opinion with an extraordinary unanimity insisting on Crispi ; those who had a claim by past position to the premiership refusing to take posts under Crispi, or, like Rudini, ready to accept only to overthrow their chief as soon as the crisis was past. The important positions were those of the Public Works, the Treasury, and the Interior, held by Crispi himself. Zanardelli, held by public opinion as too infirm in his temper, and by his extreme radical associations as well as his age, unfit for the emergency which required a nerve and promptness of decision which he did not possess, still held on to the hope of success, and, at the last moment was ready with a list, in which unfortunately for him was comprised Baratieri, the only general who could be induced to take the portfolio of War, and who by his nativity, in the Trentine, by his career as one of the Garibaldian officers transferred to the regular army, and as having been an active Irredentist, was regarded as obnoxious to Austria. This consideration compelled the King to decline giving Zanardelli the charge, which added intensity to the opposition of his group to the accession of Crispi, while making any other combination more difficult. The antagonism of the factions was never more savage than at this moment, when the insurrection in Sicily was daily gaining ground before the incompetence and panic of the acting ministry, and menaced the social order. The rival candidates were only intent on demolishing each other, while the enemy was at the gates, and almost winning in. Saracco, though not a sympathiser, much less a partisan of Crispi, but a Piedmontese of the old school of patriotism, who put the Monarchy before all other interests, accepted the invitation, with the result of bringing over the most reasonable section of the Right ; and the good-will of Sonnino, the most competent financier in the political world, carried with it a large section of the Centre. General Ricotti, the most competent military organiser, refused the invitation to take the War portfolio, it was said under pressure from the Court, and the assignment of the Treasury to Sonnino excited the most violent opposition of the extreme

Left, the leader of which, Cavallotti, distinguished in the sequence as the most rancorous enemy of Crispi, declared from his place in the Chamber that if Crispi would separate himself from Sonnino he would have no more devoted follower than himself. There was, behind the evident parliamentary crisis, a partisan struggle, the extreme Left attempting to force a ministry of a party-colour on Crispi, and the extreme Right hoping to overthrow the Crispi combination to make way for Rudini and a ministry of the Right, which should govern with the aid of the Court. Mocenni, a loyal and non-partisan soldier, accepted the portfolio of War ; Admiral Morin, the best organiser in the navy, that of the Marine, the less important positions being held by men of no eminence, and the Foreign Affairs being held *in petto* until the last moment, with the supposition that it would be held, as in Crispi's former ministry, *ad interim* by himself. It was, in fact, assigned to Baron Blanc, the former minister to Constantinople, a Senator and friend of Crispi, and as such dismissed from the diplomatic service by Rudini in 1891 under circumstances of peculiar and malignant injustice. Blanc was, beyond question, the most able and accomplished diplomat in the Italian service, and had been the private secretary of Cavour, but, having been one of the chief and most zealous advocates and workers for the Triple Alliance, was especially obnoxious to the enemies of that pact, and no doubt the reservation of his name until the completion of the ministry averted a new storm of opposition in the Chamber.

The attempt by an anarchist to assassinate Crispi, brought his popularity with the country in evidence, and he had at that time a position which, to all superficial observation, was immovable. Even the most obstinate and hostile members of the Right accepted the position as likely to last as long as Crispi lived. One heard him spoken of, even by conservative Deputies, as "minister for life," and he seemed to have inherited the position of Cavour as the indispensable man, for, in fact, there was no other statesman in view on whom the country at large placed any dependence. An ultra-conservative Deputy from the Veneto, fresh from an audience of the King, assured me that His Majesty had professed his willingness to see Crispi made Dictator. There was a concurrence of adulation from enemies of old date and perennial scoffers at the old Sicilian revolutionary, such as one could only see in Italy, but which in the condition of Italy to-day only lasted until the places to be filled were all assigned. There was a union of hearts in what concerned individual ambitions, but, the danger which had paralysed all the elements of order in the State

once gone by, the disappointed place-hunters
returned to their kennels and their sneers.

In the speech in the Chamber, which
announced the programme of the ministry as
the restoration of the finances and order, Crispi
made, in the most powerfully pathetic terms
I can remember to have heard in that House,
an appeal for the " truce of God " from party
dissensions and for union until that programme
should be attained. The response from the
majority was sceptical ; on the extreme Right
it was a laugh, on the whole discouraging,
but as Crispi had the dissolution of the
Chamber in his pocket, condition *sine qua non*
of his acceptance, he could compel respect
from an assembly, many members of which
had been elected by the corrupt pressure of
Giolitti, and could not count on a re-election.
The minister's most intimate friends and
advisers urged him to dissolve and call new
elections with no loss of time, but the old
man always replied, " I will get something
out of these." At no time since Cavour has
any Italian minister shown such a resource of
managing power, and the hostile majority,
while it accepted the old minister's deference
and conciliatory manner as symptoms of weakness, voted his measures one by one, and
mostly without modification.

In the important question of the reform
of the administration of government, involving

F. CRISPI, 1893

the necessary abolition of many places and sinecures, it was evidently impossible to secure the approbation of a majority composed as was that of the day, to the suppressions in detail, and a bill was introduced giving the ministry full powers for such reforms and abolitions of places as it regarded as necessary for administrative efficiency and economy.   To this measure I have already alluded, and it was the only one of great importance which the Chamber so modified that it was withdrawn as useless for the purposes proposed. The ministry was at that moment harmonious to an extent I can recall in no ministry in my day, and the shape of every measure was decided by the majority in Council before presentation to the Chamber, so that the usual Italian tactics of pulling a ministry to pieces like an artichoke, leaf by leaf, was impossible —a crisis meant dissolution of the Chamber, and this they did not care to face.   Other tactics became necessary.   The opposition was composed of all the corruptly elected Giolittians, that group of the extreme Right which adhered to Rudini ; all the rivals of Crispi to the succession, including Zanardelli ; those of the Left who had followed Nicotera, and some of the heads of minor groups in the Left and Centres ; but there was no agreement and no programme except to overthrow Crispi.   The rapid pacification of the

insurrection under martial law, and the check
on the deterioration of the financial position,
which obtained in the first month of the
new government under the management of
Sonnino [1] had abated the apprehensions of the
country, and it now became the habit to
minimise the past danger and Crispi's services
—it was the egg of Columbus again, and any-
body could govern as Crispi had governed.
The conspiracy took a new form, and now
there was perhaps the most curious and
characteristic display of the mediævalism
surviving in the Italian temperament which
our century has seen.   A favourite device
in the Chamber has always been to raise
a personal question, and on it to get up a
fictitious excitement, and from this to a
stampede of the undisciplined Chamber is an
easy transition.   We have seen it in the
overthrow of Crispi's first ministry ; it succeeded equally in the attack on Rudini and in
that on Giolitti, in both which cases the
ministry had a clear majority, had it been
deliberately consulted, but which gave way to
the panic and went like sheep after the leaders.
In the occasion of the new attack on Crispi,
Giolitti who, on account of the bank scandal,
was temporarily, but entirely, excluded from

[1] Sonnino admitted to me afterwards that his financial
measures would not have been carried through but for the
influence and cordial support of Crispi.

the ministerial competition, was employed as an instrument. The Radicals and Socialists took the direction of the plot, the more respectable chiefs of the constitutional opposition remaining in reserve, to fall on when the ministry should be embarrassed by the Radical attack. As fortune would have it, the Radical obstruction had so entirely blocked business for several days, that a decree of prorogation as preliminary to a dissolution had been prepared for promulgation prior to the development of the direct attack, which was to consist of a revival of the scandal of the *Banca Romana*, based on documents which Giolitti pretended to have reserved, and with which he had some time before menaced the reputations of public men unnamed, if the prosecution which had been promoted against him were not dropped. I am not disposed to blame Giolitti for the course he had taken —the persecution of him by the Radicals had been, like that of Crispi, animated by political motives entirely, and was out of all proportion to his offences, which were only an exaggeration of those common enough in Italian politics: he was under the gravamen of a political prosecution, and was evidently forced into the combination in the Chamber by the menaces of the active opposition to the ministry, and was finally compelled to put his so-called documents into the possession of

the Chamber.   The fact was that the " documents " were only empty menace ; there was
nothing in them which had not been made
public and weighed by the original Commission on the affairs of the *Banca Romana*,
but no one knew this except the principal
plotters.   The Radicals demanded a committee
for the examination of the documents ; Crispi,
with Bonghi,[1] and the temperate Deputies
not participating in the conspiracy, urged the
reference of them to the tribunal which had
possession of the charges against Giolitti ; but
the timidity of a large number of the Deputies,
who feared to be accused of being compromised by the documents if they voted
against it, decided the appointment of the
committee.   In this packet of papers, famous
since as the *Giolitti plico*, there were repeated
charges against Crispi, none of which were
new, and all of which had been weighed
and rejected by the committee on the banks,
except certain unsubstantiated imputations
made by Tanlongo, as he had promptly con-
fessed in a communication to the President
of the Chamber, under compulsion by Giolitti,
and which he afterwards admitted to be
without foundation.   The *plico* contained no
documents in evidence, or proofs of any kind

---

[1] In this crisis Bonghi, forgetting his old animosity against
his Sicilian enemy, supported the ministry with remarkable
vigour and efficacy.

of the statements made, and was legally and
morally utterly worthless, but it served to
raise the needed outcry, and the Radicals
demanded that Crispi should resign and put
himself on the defence.   The device was
transparent—Crispi out of office, there was in
the ministry no one with the prestige and
strength of hand required to sustain the continual attacks on it, and it would have been
unable, in the actual state of affairs, to hold its
own against the opposition for a week.   The
response of Crispi was the only one which
could have settled the question definitely, he
brought a libel suit against Giolitti, and as
the Chamber had become utterly anarchical,
the decree of prorogation prepared on other
grounds was issued, and the Chamber dissolved,
as it should have been long before.   The
reference of the libel to the ordinary tribunals
was opposed by Giolitti, who demanded a
trial before the Senate, and in the last resort
the majority of the Court of Appeals, on un-
questionably partisan grounds, decided that
his demand should be accorded.   The affair
was dropped as soon as the political exigency
had passed, having been in fact purely
factitious.   The constituencies pronounced
judgment in a general election which was
beyond any contradiction the freest and most
orderly held for several years, and which
supported the old Sicilian with a majority of

150 in a Chamber of 508 Deputies, not so numerous as in his former general election, but far more united, and constituted in a large measure of a class of men of an order above the usual Italian Deputy.

The question of the foreign policy has always had, from the position of Italy in Europe, a much graver importance in the stability of a ministry than in any other European country. Too weak, from the want of practical unity either in foreign or domestic interests, to stand firmly alone, successive ministries have leaned on one or the other foreign power, and have owed their stability or downfall to the power they leaned on. The energetic hostility of France towards Crispi has hardly been met by the mild, perhaps dubious, and certainly never active, influence of England, and this antagonism had a more than incidental importance in the career of this second government of Crispi. The circumstances under which he returned to power were, as I have shown, such that to all appearance he was minister during the term of his efficiency, and the French Government, recognising the policy of conciliation under the circumstances to be the only one which promised any useful results, made overtures for a reconciliation. He was offered a treaty of commerce and such financial bene-volence as Italy might be in need of, on condition that he abandoned the English understanding for the Mediterranean, propositions which in his consistent policy he refused. In this decision he made a fatal mistake, and, believing as he did in the efficiency of the English understanding, he braved the consequences of the more intense hostility of France. These consequences were the instigation of hostilities in Abyssinia and the war which resulted in the defeat at Adowah. The subsequent adhesion of the government of Crispi to the English Armenian demonstration, to support which Crispi sent the fleet to Smyrna and mobilised a *corps d'armée* for operation in Asia Minor, and the renewal of a tripartite agreement between England, Austria, and Italy, originally formed in 1887, brought Russia into the Franco-Abyssinian league with fatal consequences.

The preliminary campaign of this war was apparently a local revolt of Mangascia, the son of Giovanni, the former Negus of Abyssinia, succeeded by Menelek in alliance against Giovanni with the Italians. The campaign ended with the total defeat of Mangascia in a series of brilliant victories under the generalship of Baratieri. The revolt of Mangascia was really the opening movement of the war declared by Menelek, under the instigation of Russia and France, and the victories of Baratieri were disguised disasters, leading to overconfidence in the General and a bellicose temper in the country. Baratieri was thoroughly incompetent for anything beyond a Garibaldian movement—rash, rapid in attack and obstinate in defence, he risked total destruction in the preliminary combats where the number of the forces either of the enemy or his own troops was limited to what he held under his own eyes. Ambitious and excited by his successes, he dreamed conquests beyond his capacity to compass, and public opinion in Italy unfortunately became largely accessory to his views. Crispi was personally opposed to any extension of the operations in Africa, but he had not, as had happened to him on other occasions, the courage to oppose the popular enthusiasm and insist on the limitation of the operations to a purely defensive position within the lines then occupied. Baratieri urged an offensive defence, meeting the invasion of Menelek, which was now seen to be impending, by the occupation of the difficult country beyond the recognised frontier of the colony. Meanwhile Baratieri had been called home to explain his policy, and had given assurance that he did not require additional troops or funds, notwithstanding which the ministry sent some reinforcements. It happened that I met the General at a breakfast given by the minister of Foreign Affairs to a few friends, and an interview was given me when we left the table, in which he distinctly declared to me that his object was not to ask for reinforcements or a freer hand and extension of the territory—he did not "ask for another man or another lira" more than the modest appropriation already made, and this was based on a pacific policy, which was that desired by the Government. There was a strong suspicion in the Cabinet that these professions were insincere, and there was a disposition on the part at least of the majority of the ministers to keep the General in Italy, and send a safer man to the colony. Whether on account of a division of opinion in the Cabinet, or because the antagonism to Crispi's policy in the " unconstitutional opposition " had already begun to appear and exert an unfortunate influence on the King, I cannot say, but what is certain is that the divergence of the views of the General and the Premier were recognised by some of the political observers, for I received from the office of *The Times* communication of private information to the effect that Baratieri's object in returning was precisely the opposite of that which he declared to me and to the Government, and what was ultimately seen to be the case. The crisis was peculiar, and perhaps impossible in a strictly constitutional government, and it illustrates the difficulties under which Crispi, who was a rigid constitutionalist, always laboured. He was convinced that

Baratieri was not equal to the task before him, in case of grave complications in the colony, but from the return of the General to Massowah affairs began to grow worse. The country was exultant in the victories won, and the popularity of Baratieri was very great, and at that moment the colony enjoyed great enthusiasm over nearly the entire kingdom, and in the Chamber the suffrages were so strongly in favour of the maintenance of all that had been won that the ministry would certainly have been defeated on a proposition to withdraw before the menaced invasion by the Abyssinians. In fact, at the close of the session of Parliament preceding the fatal issue of the campaign, there was no considerable party which was willing to oppose the ministerial policy, and the order of the day which approved it was drawn up by the Marquis di Rudini, the head of the constitutional opposition, and accepted by the ministry. In the debates the only group which opposed the appropriation of 14,000,000 of lire for the colony, was the small one of the extreme Left, composed of Socialists, Republicans, and other Radicals. The Chamber adjourned in marked enthusiasm, and, with the exception of Lombardy, no part of the kingdom had maintained an opposition to the general African policy. The splendid victories of Coatit and Senafé on the south, under the immediate command of Baratieri, and those on the north under other chiefs, of Agordat, and Kassala, won against the redoubtable warriors the Abyssinians and Dervishes, had shown that the Italian military organisation and material was such as to raise the national pride to a height it had never seen since the days of San Martino, and the country at large had no misgivings as to the result of the invasion of Menelek. And the country was justified in its enthusiasms could the operations have been kept within the lines traced by the ministry.

But here begins the dolorous history of the invasion of Italy's worst enemy, the private and partisan intrigues in Court and Parliament. As may well be understood, the hostility of the enemies of Crispi in the Legislature was only masked by the assent to the general enthusiasm of the country, and the men who on one day had proposed a vote of approbation of the policy of the Government were on the next day engaged, as before, in the secret negotiations to overthrow it. The advices from Erythrea immediately after the return of Baratieri were such as to confirm in the strongest manner the distrust which Crispi had entertained of his capacity and the suspicions as to his conformity to the policy laid down for him. Crispi proposed to supersede him by Baldissera, a former Governor of the colony and a soldier of known prudence and ability, but the King refused assent, and a strong camorra was formed in the entourage of the throne, against which Crispi urged in vain, as the evidences of the incapacity and insubordination of Baratieri were brought before him, the recall of the fatal commander. Here again Crispi blundered in not offering his resignation. The information which came from most competent sources in Erythrea showed that demoralisation was increasing at such a rate in the army, that the most irresponsible favourites controlled the action of headquarters—the generals were at loggerheads and discipline rapidly disappearing. Weeks before the disaster came, letters of which I had personal cognizance warned the Government that such was the condition of the headquarters that unless some one capable of direction and maintenance of discipline came soon to take the command, a grave disaster must be looked for. Still the King refused to assent to the recall of Baratieri, and it was only when the danger was so apparent that reinforcements were sent to an extent that made the command one which, according to the regulations, a General of Baratieri's grade could no longer hold, that Baldissera was sent to take the general command. The fear was such that Baratieri, whose conduct had come to indicate either dangerous insubordination or mental deterioration, should learn of his supersession and precipitate a collison, that the orders to Baldissera were kept secret, as was supposed, and orders were sent to Massowah not to forward any letters or telegrams to Baratieri, who had gone to the front, which contained the information. The precautions were useless, for the news arrived by some secret channel, and, while Baldissera was on the way, the fatal and incredibly incompetent attack by 16,000 men on impregnable positions held by 80,000 of the finest type of savage combatants, well armed and commanded, and directed in their strategy by Russian and French officers, was made, with the result that had been apprehended by the ministry. But the demoralisation caused in the country by the defeat was a still greater disaster. The battle had been, on the part of the Italian troops, a demonstration of the splendid quality of the rank and file such as very few modern battles could show. There was no panic, though the men saw that they were in a hopeless position soon after the fighting began ; they obeyed orders as if on parade, and some brigades, whose position was hopeless, were exterminated fighting like bull-dogs, the total loss approaching 7000, the survivors retreating without panic, under the orders of the few officers left. But the losses of the Abyssinian army had been such that a renewal of the attack would have turned the face of disaster, and there were on the way and within two or

three days' call, an army larger than that which
had met Menelek at Adowah, with Baldissera
in command, and the Abyssinians were unable
to advance, while the season of the rains was
on them and a week's delay was ruin ; so that
a resolute advance by the troops at hand would
have completely changed the complexion of
affairs.   But the dismay at Rome paralysed all
operations ; as had been the case with Custozza,
Lissa, and even at Dogali, the fortitude of the
nation, government, and people, gave way
before disaster, and the enemies of Crispi, more
intent on his overthrow than on restoring the
civic courage, laboured to aggravate the panic,
and inside the ministry a division took place
which left no possibility of taking the only
remedy which was possible for the demoralisation.   The only plan of procedure which
offered a remedy was to continue the military
operations, prorogue the reopening of Parliament until the operations were concluded, and
meanwhile revive the courage of the country.
But in this juncture, Saracco, always the least
cordial of the ministers in his support of Crispi,
insisted on the convocation of Parliament,
which of course meant a defeat in the Chamber
according to all the Italian precedents, and as
his insistence would have probably been more
or less seconded by one or more other ministers,
a crisis was inevitable, and Crispi decided to
resign before meeting the Chamber.

The immediate responsibility for the disaster of Adowah lies on the King, that which fell on Crispi was owing to his reluctance to put responsibility where it belonged, and resign when the King refused assent to a measure the minister considered of vital importance. But in this case again Crispi was not well seconded by his colleagues, several of whom were unwilling to force the hand of His Majesty, and Crispi hoped by negative orders to Baratieri to compel him to refrain from offensive operations until the rains came on in Abyssinia and operation should become impossible, for Menelek was obliged to retreat before the rains began, and only two weeks lay before him when the incredible folly of Baratieri gave him his opportunity. A very singular incident at this conjuncture suggests a treason somewhere in the affair. The day before the battle took place, *La Tribuna*, the principal Roman daily, received a telegram from Tunis, communicating the news of a great disaster to the Italian army. As there was no channel of communication between Abyssinia and Tunis, the French authorities must have had some reason to anticipate a collision at that time. What is, however, of unquestionable purport is that in the intrigues of Court and the disaffected quarters of the military region, a check to the policy of Crispi in Africa was desired and, according to some Italian authorities,

expected, through the generalship of Baratieri ;
not, naturally, a grave defeat, but a sufficient
check to overthrow the ministry and discredit
the policy hitherto followed. It was even
asserted that secret orders were sent to Baratieri
to make the movement which Crispi had
forbidden, and there was this ground for the
suspicion, that a General who was sent out to
reinforce Baratieri on the eve of the battle was
one of those most hostile to Crispi, in the
hostile army circles. The impression left on
my own mind, being more or less in knowledge of what was going on, was that the opposition to Crispi personally was maintained
in the War Office (outside the Cabinet of the
minister, Mocenni, who was a loyal soldier),
and by the King and the circle around him.
But the policy in Africa was not the policy
of Crispi, who had from the beginning opposed the colony, and only accepted it when
he considered the honour of the flag compromised. The only occasion on which I
had ever offered an opinion on the policy of
the Government to Crispi was when he came
to the ministry in 1893, and when making the
usual visit of congratulation. I then expressed
the hope that he would abandon the African
colony, and obey his original forebodings of
disaster. He replied that the honour of Italy
was engaged and it was impossible to withdraw.
"We have had the sacrifices," he said, " and

now we must realise the profits." For myself I could never anticipate any profits, and the colony always portended sacrifice to the end.

The political situation at the moment of the battle of Adowah is a most instructive picture of the condition of Italian politics, and will explain the pessimism with which the well-informed student of them regards the future of the kingdom. Against the ministry, headed by the admittedly most competent man in the country, comprising several of the most honest and able administrators, Sonnino, Maggiorino Ferraris, Blanc in Foreign Affairs, Saracco, who, if hardly ever a cordial supporter of Crispi, was a minister of the most unimpeachable integrity and capacity in administration, and with colleagues without exception of unquestioned uprightness, all the occult forces of the kingdom were arrayed. The King himself might have given the ministry a solid position had he been acting in cordial good faith towards Crispi, but he was not. He sheltered the intrigues of the Court and the element in the army hostile to Crispi, and these, as well as the chiefs of the groups in the opposition in the Chamber, were willing to risk a check in Africa to secure the overthrow of a minister whom they all hated ; in the ministry a majority were opposed to forcing the hand of the King, and of this majority Crispi was

himself a member; he seemed to have developed in his old age a clinging to office,
and abandoned the independence of his earlier
career, while every measure by which he
wished to secure the solidity of his own and
the ministry's position met a strong and un-
yielding passive opposition in quarters which
inevitably affected the Parliamentary position, — secret hostility surrounded him, and
he was even only supported loyally by an
actual minority, a large one, however, of the
Chamber; the Senate, always ready to follow
a signal of the King, was lukewarm in support
of the Government, and only the old parliamentary hand's knowledge of tactics enabled
him to meet the difficulties of the position
for a time.   Crispi himself obeyed the exigencies of the situation in all loyalty — his
great difficulty had always been in his personal
surroundings and domestic intrusion in public
affairs, but every attempt at such intrusion
in appointments or measures met the firm
opposition of the ministry, in which his own
concurred.   Certain nominations, due to such
influences, showed the real and grave weakness
of Crispi in public affairs, and against these
his colleagues were united, and he invariably
accepted the decisions of the majority.   There
is no more pathetic history in the annals of
constitutional government than that of the
end of Crispi's official career.   Hated on the

one hand by all the friends of antiquated privilege, by the Church and all its reactionary allies and the stagnant elements of the conservative order of things, on the other he was even more cordially detested by the propagators of disorder and radical dissolution of the state, and the object of all the political hostility of the successive governments of France ; and beyond and around all this positive antagonism, he was opposed by the lethargy and indifference of the Italian political stagnation, annoyed by his nervous activity and insistence ; but his chief, because most intimate, enemies were those of his own household, against which he had no defence.

The fiery and aggressive temper in which, in his career as head of the party of action, he had sown the seeds of life-long hostilities, had changed to the politic and conciliatory, even to humble solicitation to old enemies to join him in effort to heal and save the State, to be met always by the factious and irreconcilable rancours of a generation gone by. During his first premiership, when the corruption in the magistracy called for reforms, he organised a section in the Council of State for the supervision of the Bench, and put at the head of it Silvio Spaventa, a political opponent, but a man of the most unimpeachable integrity. In this, as in other cases, where he acted on motives of the highest regard for the good of the State, without thought of his party connections, his action brought on him the animosity of his partisans without conciliating in the least his opponents. In such surroundings, political and social, the fall of such a minister is always imminent. The nature of the man is incompatible with office in a country disorganised and chaotic as is Italy, and while he walked in good faith and respect for the constitution, there was no moment when a new snare was not being spread for him.

A possible partial cause of the King's defection from his minister, may be found in the fact, that soon after Crispi came to power in 1893 he notified the German Government of his intention to denounce the treaty of the Triple Alliance, to secure in new negotiations the protection for the African interests of Italy more satisfactorily than they had been arranged in the earlier treaty. This the Kaiser resented, and sent word to the King that Crispi was becoming importunate, and must be got rid of. No proof can be offered that this recommendation weighed as imperative with the King, but it is highly improbable that it should not have strengthened the Court influence, always hostile to Crispi.

The return of the enemies of Crispi to power was the signal for the renewal of the partisan war which had been interrupted by the Sicilian troubles, and an effort was made to implicate him in irregularities in the management of the Bank of Naples, the Director of which was accused of peculations, and who in his defence alleged the participation of Crispi in the operations which were the occasion of the irregularities. The Commission *ad hoc* found that Crispi had not been an accomplice in those irregularities, but that he had in unwise friendship for the Director countermanded an inquiry into the condition of the bank, by which the latter hoped to be enabled to restore the balance against him. The case against the Director is still pending in the Italian courts, and includes a charge of participation by Signora Crispi. The fair conclusion is in agreement with the opinion of all who have known Crispi in his official relations, viz. that though incapable of peculation himself, he has always been surrounded by people who made use of his name and influence to commit irregularities, and sometimes illegalities, profiting by his confidence in them. He is notoriously a bad judge of professed friends, and the worst mistakes of his official career have been committed through mistaken confidence in men who only became his partisans for corrupt purposes. The domestic relations of his later life have been disastrous, but a tolerably thorough knowledge of the circumstances enable me to say that his misfortunes have come on him more by the agency of others than by his own conduct. The testimony of those who have known him longest and best in his political career is that he is incapable of using his official position for his pecuniary advantage, and the fact that, after six years of his tenure of the Premiership, the original debt with which he entered office with Depretis was unpaid when he fell in 1895, is proof presumptive that he had not profited by office. And the man who refused advancement and competence under Cavour rather than disavow his political principles, who under Garibaldi refused all stipend and had to be pecuniarily assisted to reach Turin, after having administered the affairs of a kingdom, and who repelled office for nearly twenty years, can hardly be justly accused, except on indubitable evidence, of official dishonesty, and now that he is no longer on the way to power, but a broken and nearly blind old man, even his enemies might be content to let justice be done him. The defects of his temperament have made him many enemies and left him few friends, but he is the last of the men who made Italy, and who in their official position have always had a distinct and consistent programme of policy, home and foreign. At the age of eighty he passes out of practical politics, not from mental infirmities, for his mind seems as vigorous as ever, but his physical condition renders him unfit for the devotion to official duties which is necessary in an organisation so chaotic as that of Italy. All the heads of groups in the Chamber regard him as an obstacle to their advancement, for his position is not one that will fall into a second place, and every combination of groups will be formed on the exclusion of him from the ministry, not necessarily from hostility, but because no one of the leaders would yield to him the first place. He is a solitary survival of an epoch when there were giants in the land, where now only respectable and inoffensive mediocrity can be permitted to preside. The public opinion in Italy no longer desires a living and growing Italy—it gradually but surely glides in the wake of Spain and Portugal, and a man like Crispi, with ambitions for the assignment of a rôle amongst the powers, such as a nation with a population of thirty millions has a right to take, is out of place. His activity is antipathetic to the national apathy, and, as I have often heard it said, " he is too big for Italy." This, and nothing else is at the bottom of the hostility felt for him in the better classes of the Italian people. Amongst the masses at large he is the only man in politics who is capable of exciting any enthusiasm, because the people, living as it does under the social oppression of the wealthy classes, and being at heart a good and docile people, feels the need of a strong authority able to correct abuses. Italy

will build him a monument, and amongst those
who will be most eager to decree it will be
those who most feared and assailed him when
living.

The charge of megalomania against Crispi
has only the basis, that he always insisted
that Italy should take her position amongst the
powers as a nation of thirty millions of people
ought, and that the position which Cavour
placed her in should be maintained, as one of
the active powers of Europe, with rights and
obligations as to the general condition, under
the alternative of declining with Spain and
Portugal. The result of the last ten years is
to show, even him, that his was an idle dream.
Italy is incapable of any foreign policy but that
of a protected power. Civic virtue is at too
low an ebb for the nation to have any active
policy. The conflict of personal ambitions has
eaten up the general well-being of its Government ; corruption in its legislative and judicial
regions, increasing rather than diminishing, has
destroyed the confidence of the masses, which
is the main strength of every good government.
Crispi's dream was an idle one, and perhaps his
greatest sorrow is to see his disillusion.

APPENDIX

REPUBLIC *VERSUS* MONARCHY

A Letter to Giuseppe Mazzini

TURIN, 18*th March* 1865.

THE only reason which induces me to answer the letter addressed to me, which was printed in the *Unità Italiana* of the 3rd of January, is that it is yours. But I shall not follow your example; I shall write in a friendly spirit, although you have declared through the press that all friendship has ceased between us.

I do not mean to inquire into the motives that induced the Deputy Mordini, on the 18th of November 1864, to make the declaration to the Chamber which provoked me to give the answer you have so bitterly censured. I know that what I said came from my heart, and I was convinced then, as I am now, that the maxims I then proclaimed in the Chamber would be salutary to Italy.

Yes! *Monarchy unites us, while a Republic would separate us;* and to think otherwise is not to know our country nor the conditions of Europe.

If the cry of republic were to be raised in a southern city it would not find an echo; were it

Q

even to be accepted there, it would not extend beyond the place in which it was raised. I will say even more, if that cry were to triumph even in one or more provinces of the state, were it to spread over all the territory beyond the Tronto, it would not be repeated by the population of the centre of the peninsula, and would be repelled by those of the north.

You would see the nucleus of twenty-two millions of Italians composing the new kingdom divided ; you would see the failure of that national unity which is your and our desire, and which ought to be the glory of our generation.

I wish to be liberal in my conceptions. I am ready to admit (you see I even exceed your desires) that the Piedmontese, who are devoted to the house of Savoy, would overthrow it, and that the Lombards, so especially conservative now, in presence of the threatening Austrians on the other side of the Mincio, would fraternise with the republicans of Turin. I will add to this still another dream ; I will allow that the Tuscans, who in 1849, under the guidance of Guerazzi, refused to be united to Rome, would accept a republic ; and that in Florence, in the Hall of the Cinquecento, the national assembly would gather together, and that the triumvirate would have its seat in the Pitti Palace. But what would be the consequences ?

The Republic could not live without expanding beyond the Alps. All understand this, and our enemies better than any.

The French Republic of 1793 only existed under similar conditions.

The principles through which the new Government would exist would put us at variance with all the monarchs of the old continent. Napoleon would increase his troops in Rome and in Savoy, and before a single Italian soldier could pass beyond Ventimiglia or the Mont Cenis the French troops would occupy Naples and Piedmont.

On this occasion also, as in 1849, the Hapsburgs would act in union with Bonaparte, and, crossing the Po, would go straight to Florence. The English would invest Sicily to hold a pledge in view of future diplomatic combinations, or would look on impassibly at the occupation of our territory, as they did recently for Denmark.

We should be subject to a treaty even worse than that of Zurich.

The Republic would be dissolved, with our unity.

Concede me another hypothesis.

Let us suppose that, leaving aside for the moment the kingdom of Italy, you concentrate your efforts on Rome and Venice, with the aim of successfully creating a Republic in either of those cities, in order to extend it over the remainder of Italy.

In Rome, for instance ?

But the French are there still, and, unfortunately, behind the garrison commanded by the Duke of Montebello all France stands ready to fly to the defence of her own flag.

The 30th of April 1849 the Romans, with valour equal to their ancestors, repelled the invasion. And what came of it ? The number and means of the enemy's army were increased, and, notwithstanding the valour of our young soldiers, the defence had to be given up, and the political papacy was restored in a still more cruel form than before. Your attempts to organise an insurrection on 3rd July 1849 were vain, and in the following sixteen years the most impetuous among its young men were sent into exile, or condemned to hard labour, and no movement took place indicating the awakening of the eternal city.

In Venice, then? The events of Friuli are still fresh in every memory. Those generous creatures fighting there quite recently did not pronounce the word republic, although your own inspiration and advice did not fail them. And they were right, for with that word they would have closed the way to the help they hoped for from the kingdom of Italy. You yourself, when writing to them before they began to fight, declared that their cry could only be for monarchy.

In any way, let us suppose all obstacles overcome, and that in one of these cities the Republic should obtain an easy victory. When the moment came to extend its dominion, without having simultaneously upset, with other revolutions, the great monarchies beyond the Alps, the Republic would have opposed to it the army of the Italian kingdom and, behind it or with it, the Austrian and the French. I need not observe to you that the Republic in the midst of our populations would sow the germs of that discord which we have always sought to avoid, and by which the reaction would profit. Most assuredly before its advent our forces would be disorganised, and before they could be reorganised our enemies would have time to prevent the constitution of our national unity.

To all this I foresee your answer. You will doubtless say that I have no longer faith in our people, that I have not faith in the revolution and in the progress of humanity.

I am as bold as ever, and you have good proof of

it. You do not ignore that I did not throw myself into politics out of despair, or to make a living out of them, but through deep and certain convictions. If all believed as I do, and were as ready to act, things would go differently. In the last four years I have had much experience of men ; and through too great impatience I do not wish to repeat the fable of the dog who, crossing the river with the meat in his mouth, miserably duped, let it fall in the water to catch the shadow.

You are a republican.
You say so ; I believe you.
But you are not of the same stuff as those re-publicans of the Convention who refused to treat with the King. In 1831, when you stepped into active politics, your first thought was for Carlo Alberto, to whom you offered your services, if only he would put himself at the head of the nation.
" Unite us, Sire," you said, " we will gather round you ; we offer you our lives, and we will lead under your banners all the small Italian states."
Fifteen years of conspiracies, martyrdoms, of un-fortunate movements, and of glorious achievements elapsed. Saluted by people in slavery, who always hope in the advent of every new prince, Pius IX. came to the papacy, and even you thought from what he said that he was able to bring about the unification of our country. On the 8th of September 1847 you wrote him a letter which, after having been put in the Pontiff's hands, made the round of Europe. From it, it will suffice me to quote your counsels and the expression of your faith.
" Unify Italy, your country, and to this end you have no need to do more than to bless those who

work for you in your name. We will make a nation
to rise up around you whose free and popular development you will preside over during your lifetime. We will found a unique Government in the
midst of Europe which shall destroy the absurd
divorce between spiritual and temporal power, and
in which you will be chosen to represent the principle
to which the men called to represent the nation will
make the applications."

Not finding a king to make one family out of
the nation, you invoked theocracy, which, being the
destruction of all liberty of conscience, is also the
destruction of all liberty. But your words were not
listened to, and the regeneration of Italy began by
the initiative of a city from a spot where it was least
expected. In January 1848 Palermo rose with admirable intrepidity, and later, in March, Milan. As
if touched by an electric current, the whole peninsula
was in arms, and almost seemed to overcome the
invaders. The astonishing action of our people did
not bring about unity immediately, but made the
desire for it general ; and after the Homeric struggles
of Venice and of Rome it became known to our
friends, as well as to our enemies, that there existed
a force in the country, till then unknown, which
sooner or later must emancipate us.

The honour of Rome's resistance to the French is
due in great measure to yourself. Was not the
Roman Republic due to you, though proclaimed
twenty-five days before you arrived in the eternal city ?

You certainly cannot say that from 1848 to 1849,
during the War of Independence, your republican
heart did not believe for an instant in monarchy for
the redemption of Italian unity.

In a programme published at that juncture you

wrote that your desire was, first, emancipation from foreign rule ; second, the unification of the fatherland, without which independence would only be illusory ; and third, the form, the institution, which should assure the preservation of its liberty and the mission of civilisation in our country, but on this point you promised not to be intolerant, and that you would be ready to be silent concerning the Republic if the independence and unification of Italy should come from the principality.

The chances of war becoming unfavourable in Lombardy a friend of yours came to you with a message from the camp. Your opinion being asked as to how the difficulties could be overcome and the forces of all parties united in the war against Austria, you proposed a proclamation in which the King should manifest in the following terms his plan :—

"I feel that the moment has come for the unity of our country. I understand, oh Italians ! the impatience that grieves your very souls. Up, then, rise, I will go before you. Behold, I pledge my faith to you ; I offer a spectacle the world has not known, of a King, the high priest of a new epoch, an armed apostle of the idea of the people who himself rears the temple of the nation. I break in God's name, and in that of Italy, those old bonds which hold you dismembered and are rusty with your blood. I call upon you to overthrow the barriers which keep you divided even to-day, and to collect together legions of free brothers emancipated around me, your leader, ready to fall or to conquer with you."

This proposal from you was not accepted, as you yourself wrote later in the *Italia del Popolo*, which was published at Lausanne. It was not you who

objected to the King, but the King who would not
have compacts with you.

The revolution being unsuccessful, all good patriots
took the road of exile. You returned to England
and constituted the national committee, assembling
around you in London, Saliceti, Sirtori, Montecchi,
and Quadrio ; in Paris, Amari and La Farina ; in
Piedmont, Bertani, myself, and Rosalino Pilo ; others
also in other cities. You presented yourself to the
Italians with the proclamation of September 1850,
in which were those words :—

"Italy desires to be one nation for her own sake
and that of others, as much by right as by duty.
She desires to be united not in the manner of a
Napoleonic unity, with an exaggerated administrative
centralisation that deprives the constituent parts of
the nation of their liberty to the advantage of the
capital, but to be united by her constitution, her
assembly interpreting the constitution, to be united
by her international relations, by her army, her code,
and her education.   And in order to become a nation
it is necessary she should acquire by action and by
sacrifice the consciousness of her duties and of her
rights.

"A war comprising all her regular and irregular
forces, commanded by men of proved patriotism,
directed by one supreme authority, having no obligation but that of victory, no hope but that which is
obtained by a serene and strong conscience, no confidence but in struggle, can bring about the well-being
of Italy.

"Does any Government exist willing to adopt
this programme — a Government that, with the
people and for the people, would make a war without

any concession to privileges, prejudices, internal differences, and foreign usurpers? Let such a Government declare itself, and our united forces will come to its aid."

The Government to which you made this appeal could be neither the Austrian, nor that of the Grand Dukes, nor that of the Bourbons, nor that of the Pontiff. The Government to which you appealed was the Piedmontese, and was not of the people, but had Vittorio Emanuele for its head.

The committee only lasted long enough to make a national loan, because your companions—for reasons which I choose to ignore—all abandoned you. Then came the gallows of February 1853, the torture and deaths of Malano and Bentivegna, the memorable expedition of Sapri, to which are connected the ill-advised attempt at Genoa and the bloody struggles of Leghorn.

Our party for several years had no success whatever; but we did not therefore weary or lose faith in ourselves. The image of national unity was before us with most flattering hopes, and in order to secure her we returned to face death. Nor think that our energy has become lessened, and that our heart to-day is deaf to the voice of sacrifice. This miserable life would be a burden to us if we had to endure it dishonoured, and not make use of it for our country.

On the 30th of April 1859 the war with Austria broke out. The manner in which it began made us fear that a new bondage would come of it for Italy; so that many of our party abstained from taking part in it, but continued the propaganda of ideas to educate the nation in the sense of its own duties.

On the following 12th of July the royal and imperial chiefs decided at Villafranca, that our country should be made into a confederacy of princes with the Pope at its head, and the Emperor of Austria as one of its members. It was then we considered the moment ripe for leaving the land of exile and throwing ourselves among our people to prevent this project of diplomacy from taking effect, and to hasten the constitution of the national unity by making use of the elements offered us by the various provinces.

From Tuscany, the Grand Duke had been gone since the 27th of April, and the necessities of war having called the Austrians away, all the territory which extends from Piacenza to the Cattolica remained under the charge of its citizens. In view of the preliminaries of peace of the two emperors, Farini by an act of far-seeking audacity, for which the nation must ever be grateful to him, breaking every link with the Sardinian Government, accepted the Dictatorship in the duchies and then extended it over Romagna. A provisional government had already formed itself at Florence. The Marches and Umbria were fermenting, and the southern provinces appeared by several signs to be intolerant of the Bourbon rule.

In this state of affairs, what were your intentions? What was your banner?

No one thought of excluding the kingdom in order to constitute the nation. Convinced that the King by the new alliance and by the treaties was obliged not to violate the conditions of the armistice, we decided to adopt independent action without him, for the achievement of the national unity, although we were not inimical to him. We agreed to excite the provinces of the peninsula which were still in thraldom to a general insurrection, and to fight together for the formation of a new kingdom.

With this aim I left for Sicily, and you a few days after went into Tuscany, and did your utmost that the provinces that were already free should unite themselves to Piedmont.

In 1858 the *Italia e Popolo* of Genoa published some of your articles, in which the nation's continuous progress towards unity was delineated. You intended to show how the fusion of different races in our country had come about, and how the indigenous race had always absorbed the others. In the article published on the 25th of February, were these words :—"The islands of Italy alone offer a really distinct physiognomy ; that is why a national government would not refuse them a special administration."

I do not discuss whether our islands have a really distinct character. I know that the Latin element supersedes all others in the continual combinations of different races which repeated invasions brought about. I also know certainly that they lived under their own laws, with their own peculiar customs, and separated as they were from the continent, they kept up an autonomy not easily to be destroyed.

In Sicily, after the restoration of the Bourbons, the political parties contending for ascendency were two, our own, the unitarian, and that of the autonomists. In the midst of these, after 1858 a third sprung up, declaring itself openly inimical to us, although like ourselves desiring unity ; this party made the people hope for help from the Sardinian Government, a deception which diminished their faith in their own strength. The monarchical separatists were supported by individuals in exile ; but at home they had only with them certain literary

men attached to the traditions of 1812. Their
authority did not extend over the people, who
having been left in May 1849 to the care of the
Usurper, only believed in us, for they had seen us
since 1848 always in posts of danger, at the
barricades, and in prison.

The battles of Palestro and San Martino had
extended the influence of the third party, afterwards
called the Piedmontese. There were some of them
who declared, and others who believed, that Vittorio
Emanuele was ready to make war on Francis II.,
and that Sicily would be liberated as Lombardy had
been.

All this you knew, and your judgment was too
sound for you to talk of a republic here. The wind
was blowing in favour of monarchy, and to combat
it openly or to propose ideas immediately hostile to
it would have created fresh perils for unity, the
realisation of which was opposed by all the Cabinets
of Europe. Our business was to dissipate the false
hopes which were putting to sleep the unfortunate
people, and took from them the consciousness of
their own strength.

The 9th of July 1859 I made preparations for
my journey. You, in a piece of paper which you
sent me to Malden Terrace, sketched the situation,
such as I should declare it to be to our friends in
Sicily.

"Revolution in the four Italies if the war should
be followed up with obstinancy—in five or six if
peace concludes on the Mincio with a treaty of
Plombieres. All the circumstances which took place
afterwards accorded with this sketch.

"Sicily would not be considered except through
the success of the Murat Combination.

"At the end of the war, the allies would limit themselves to insisting with the King of Naples that he should bring about some reforms which would stifle for a time the revolutionary movement.

"The unity of Italy would be out of the question. The King may desire it secretly, but never achieve it.

"Sicily had, therefore, nothing to hope for from Piedmont. To follow blindly its instructions means finding herself one day so placed that she can do absolutely nothing, for at the conclusion of the war, the *status quo* which will be insisted on for the south and part of the centre will be guaranteed by the European governments. If Sicily therefore desires liberty and to be united, she must have recourse to insurrection. Let her have recourse without delay to insurrection so that the negotiations which are to take place should not ignore her."

These words comprise more than a programme. When on my return from Palermo I prepared myself for a second journey in the island, you were even more explicit in your ideas. A letter to me of the 16th of September proves this : the King was then prevented by international policy from accepting the oaths from the national assemblies of Emilia and Tuscany. This event did not change your mind and make you turn against the kingdom. The Republic was not in your project because it would have been an impediment to unity. "If there is no way," you wrote to me, "to avoid their offering themselves to the kindgom, at least let it be done with dignity, for unconditional acceptance, *yes* or *no.*"

Finally, on the 2nd of March 1860, all doubts ceased ; your language was more frankly explicit.

In a letter to our friends of Palermo and of Messina you made this declaration :—

"I repeat to you what we have been printing for the last two years. *It is no longer a question whether we should have a Republic or a Monarchy: the question is national unity—to be or not to be*—to remain dismembered and slaves to the will of a foreign despot whether French or Austrian, or to be *ourselves,* to be men, to be free, to be considered as such, and not as children in leading strings, as incapable by the whole of Europe. If Italy desire to *become a Monarchy under* the House of Savoy, let it be so. If afterwards she wishes to hail *as her liberators or whatever else she may please to call them, the King and Cavour, let her do so.* What we all wish now is that Italy should be made."

Nor could you hold a different language, since you were speaking to a people who for eight centuries had been monarchical, and who, according to one of your own phrases quoted above, *offered a quite exceptional physiognomy.* The same moderation inspired you when in London, the 20th of February 1848, you acclaimed our victories. You did not accuse us then of not having chosen a government of the people ; you only imputed it as an error of the victorious island that had rebelled against Bourbon rule, that it wished to separate itself from the continent, and to divide the kingdom of the two Sicilies. In the fever for national unity, you gave us an example of patriotic strength forgetting your native city, and calling the act of the Congress of Vienna, which had handed Genoa over to the King of Sardinia, *providential.* It is proper here to repeat your own words to the Sicilians.

" You form to-day an important and vital part of

the most populous state of Italy, the strongest as regards position, ships, and arms. The first to raise the cry of liberty, the first to be triumphant, saluted by the hearty admiration of your fellow-citizens on *terra firma*, you have acquired an influence that will not die, a novel power that none wish, or can, dispute you—rights that none will, however, seek to deprive you of. Why should you diminish your strength and that of your fellow-citizens by separating yourselves from them? Why should you renounce by voluntary suicide the rank which, when united, you can occupy in Europe, to descend to the fourth, the last rank, condemning yourselves to continual weakness and to inevitable foreign influence? It is because the Government of Naples has oppressed you for so long and treated you as though you were a colony. But did not the same tyranny weigh on your brother citizens of the mainland?

"Did they not abhor it? do they not still abhor it as you abhor it? Did they not protest by conspiracies, by secret societies, by the blood of the noblest among them? Were not your executioners those also of the Neapolitans? Were there not between you and the men of Calabria oftentimes solemn compacts of insurrection? Did not these compacts make a solemn manifestation in the face of all Europe by the banner raised between August and September 1847 in the brief space of forty-eight hours in Reggio and in Messina? Ah! do not forget, oh Sicilians! the alliance that the martyrs of Reggio, of Messina, and of Gerace signed with their blood. Do not betray in time of victory the holy promises made during the battle. Be now and ever brethren according to your oath. Do not act so that the foreigner may say exultingly—*Free they may become, but strong and united, never!*   You have taught Italy the power of will ; teach her the holiness of love ; teach her the religion of unity, which alone can give her glory, a mission, and free action for the third time in Europe.

"I am not a Neapolitan.   I was born in Genoa, also a great city once upon a time, through its own free and independent life : great also for having given in 1746 to slumbering Italy the last example of manly courage, as you have now given the first example to awakened Italy.   Like yourselves, we were in 1815 given, without our consent, to another Italian state, whose memories of the past embittered our relations, and from whom we had received for many years more injuries than benefits, as often happens in a union not freely chosen, but decreed by foreign interference.   And, nevertheless, those amongst us who loved one common fatherland had so much desire and confidence in the future that they hailed this union as providential."

The secret work of the conspirators bore its fruit. On the 4th April 1860 Palermo was in revolt. The movement was suffocated in blood in the city itself, but spread in the surrounding country, and survived there.   Garibaldi had declared as early as February that he would lend to Sicily the valuable help of his sword.   Repeating his promise to Rosalino Pilo in a letter of the 15th of March, he expressed himself thus :—"In case of action, remember that the programme is : Italy and Vittorio Emanuele." Rosalino, when he answered him, did not refuse this programme, and went before us on the road to Messina.   The 5th of May we left Quarto ; you had been forewarned of this plan through two letters and a telegram from Turin. It was not your fault if you did not come; I learned afterwards that you had been ill, and arrived in Genoa two days after our departure. On the 7th of May, on board the *Piemonte*, Captain Bruzzesi read to the volunteers the first order of the day, concluding thus : " The war-cry of the ' cacciatori dei alpi,' the military organisation of the northern province of Italy formed under Garibaldi's directions, is the same as that which sounded on the banks of the Ticino twelve months ago : ' Italy and Vittorio Emanuele ' ; and this cry, although from our lips, will strike terror among the enemies of Italy." Brusco Onis alone felt hurt in his republican soul by this monarchical programme, and when we touched at Talamone he left the steamer, and was not seen again. The brothers Mosto, Savi, and other of our friends remained at their post, convinced that it was impossible to discuss the form of government, as men ready to give their own lives in order to give life to the nation. On the 11th of May we landed at Marsala, and the 13th we arrived at Salemi, where on the morrow the dictatorship was proclaimed in the name of the King of Italy. On the 15th we were victorious at Calatafimi, and the banner to which Schiaffino clung when he was dying, and which was lacerated by the enemies' balls, had in its centre the image of Italy resting her right hand on the shield of Savoy. On the 17th the organic decrees of the new Government were published, and from that moment the sentences and all public acts were proclaimed in the King's name, and these were headed, as were the laws of the dictatorship, by the arms of the Italian Royal House. The intentions of the new authority could no longer be doubted ; and after serious obstacles on the mountains around

Palermo, on the 27th of March it entered the capital of the island acclaimed by the people and the bombardment of the Bourbons.

I will not recall the details of those memorable days. The whole country came to our help, and from all parts of Italy arrived subsidies, so that the undertaking for national redemption should be successful. On the 20th of July, after a severe encounter, we became masters of Milazzo ; on the 27th, of Messina ; and Sicily thus freed, the first volunteers on the night of the 8th of August could pass over the Faro. On the continent the revolution fell like an avalanche on the throne of the Bourbons. Acclaimed by all as a liberator on the 7th of September, Garibaldi, unarmed and with few friends, made his entrance into Naples. On the 2nd of October the hero defeated the last army of the tyrants on the Volturno. On the 21st of the same month the kingdom of the two Sicilies was no more, and from the electoral urn the plebiscite declared, in the face of the world, Italy one and indivisible with Vittorio Emanuele its constitutional King.

Four months later the representatives of nine-tenths of the nation assembled in Parliament.

In the brief space of time during which so much was accomplished, you raised no word for the Republic. Certainly that would have been the moment to have held up the people's banner, and to censure your friends, who being in power had pledged themselves to monarchy. But you, in 1860 as in 1831, as also in 1848 and in 1859, always insisted that form should be sacrificed before that great idol of the unity of a complete nation. You understood that if in Sicily or on Neapolitan territory the Phyrgian cap had been raised, a fatal division in the peninsula would have ensued, and we should only have prepared for the restoration of the fallen princes. In all the letters that I received from you, from June to August 1860, I only find praise. "The Sicilians," you wrote on the 9th of June, "God help them for ever, have given for the second time, as a people, a glorious initiative. If Italy knows how to make use of it, they will have saved Italy. But their example must be followed, and we will follow it." Your repugnance and your fears were not for the Monarchy of Vittorio Émanuele. That which very justly occupied your mind was the danger of a federation which was to be opposed at any cost. You held in Naples as in Palermo the autonomists to be our enemies and not the Piedmontese. In a few lines of the 17th of June you expressed yourself thus :—

"Through the kingdom serious movements threaten us, concessions of constitutions, etc. Heaven forbid this should happen to us! Farewell for ever to unity. It is, therefore, necessary to hasten the assault of the kingdom on our own account."

And in the letter of the 22nd of June, with reference to the risings in Sicily! "If you are sure of remaining in power, you should prolong as much as possible the provisional government, until the whole kingdom has been freed. . . . If you are not sure of remaining in power, that is another thing. Then rather than allow the Independents to have a footing, hasten suffrage and an assembly." And on the same occasion, greeting Nicola Fabrizzi on his arrival in the island, you wrote to him : "If the autonomists agitate, hurry on annexation." You were then so far from combating the Monarchy so closely allied to the accomplishment of our unity, that when invited to come to Sicily, you wrote to Savi and Mosto the 19th of June:

"Since I could not come before the movement, I shall not come to Sicily. I am tired of being misunderstood; seeing me at this moment people would say I came to work against Garibaldi, or heaven knows what."

And you were right! No one believed that in the interests of unity you would not even have attacked the Monarchy. I believed you would not, because your whole life was impressed on my mind, and my heart bled to think the country should misunderstand you, and forgetting your virtues would be ungrateful to you.

The Dictatorship being established in Naples, it was our duty to give organic power and unity to the revolution in the south, so as to complete the mission for which we had taken up arms, by its strength. All our efforts converged towards this end, and it was the common belief that our success would have been impossible if we had risen inimical to the King, who a year before had unsheathed his sword in the name of Italy, and in whom the provinces not yet redeemed hoped, since the recent annexations. The 16th of September 1860 Garibaldi declared that, being obliged to go away from the southern provinces, he had delegated the Government of Naples and that of Sicily to two Prodictators, only retaining for himself the legislative power and the supreme direction of military and political affairs. To put his decision into effect, he decreed that in the interests of both parts of the former kingdom, two Secretaries of State should be

with him, to whom should be entrusted the portfolios
of Foreign Affairs and of War. From that moment,
this organisation of the Dictatorship made our
intentions clear ; Garibaldi had made no mystery
about them in a proclamation of the 11th of
September to the people of Palermo. In this, one
might read " The annexation to the kingdom of the
Re Galantuomo we shall soon proclaim from the
summit of the Quirinal," an idea more clearly
manifested in the brief and exciting speech he pronounced himself to the people on the 17th, from
the balcony of the Norman Royal Palace : " To this
people," he said, " I must give thanks ; to you people of
Palermo, to whom I am bound by having shared
with you fatigue, danger, and glory, to you, brave
people, who, trusting in me, did not allow yourselves
to be led away to too early annexation ! If annexation had been made two months ago I should not
have crossed the Strait. If those who sought to
deceive you had been listened to, we should have
been in bondage through diplomacy. Also in Naples
some partisans of annexation arose, but I opposed
myself to them, and the people of that illustrious city
put faith in my word, while the whole of Italy is
not free ; while our brothers beyond the Volturno
remain with the chain about their feet we will fight."
To many, and to some of our own party, so much
audacity seemed imprudent. Nevertheless, if Italy
ever had a propitious moment, it was that one, and
unfortunately we let it go by. There our opponents
were defeated and dared not raise their head.
Austria had not recovered by any means from the
defeats suffered in 1859 ; and terrified, uncertain,
powerless against us were the princes that the revolution had deprived of their thrones. France on her

side was suffering from the battles fought on Lombard soil ; and even if the Emperor had assembled a new army, he could not have used it to our destruction. In Paris, the name of Garibaldi was popular through the wonders achieved that year ; and among the workmen and soldiers the echo of that voice which proclaimed the liberation of the peninsula from the Alps to the Adriatic still sounded. In any case after the cession of Nice and Savoy, for Napoleon to take up arms again would have been the signal for a European war all were anxious to avoid. The great powers felt in their hearts the duty of remaining neutral towards Italy, and there is proof of a refusal of England to intervene in the Strait of Messina to prevent our volunteers disembarking on the continent. Against the consummation of our plans, difficulties arose on every side. In Palermo, they complained that we had deprived the local government of all liberty of action, and Signor Friscia, now a Deputy, was sent to Garibaldi to advocate Sicilian autonomy. In Naples there was worse ; a party of intriguers, incapable of governing the country, had insinuated themselves into public posts to put difficulties in the way of the movements of those in power, and to prevent the organisation of the army. And in the island, as also on the mainland, public opinion was put on a false track by incessant street rows and a perfidious press, so that the coming of the King was longed for as a necessary termination to such unsteady administration, to which views and abuses were falsely imputed. In this moment in which the different parties were conspiring to harass the Government in the transaction of public affairs, and to bar the road which would have led us to Rome, what

was your proposal? What did you ask of your
friends? Did you think of the Republic at all?
Did you dictate it as the only way that could put
the people on the right path and would prevent
the turncoats come from Turin from having any
advantage over us? Nothing of the kind. You
had but one thought, that of overcoming the
suspicion and diffidence which assailed you and your
friends. You published, meanwhile, in the *Iride*, a
Neapolitan journal, a declaration, so that the world
should know that a republic was out of the question
in the great movement towards national unity, and
that the republicans, come to fight in the southern
provinces, had accepted the monarchical programme
of Garibaldi.

"On what basis," you exclaimed, "are the
suspicions founded which are accumulating against
the republicans? Although I have investigated
carefully, I have not found any accusation that is
not an absurd calumny, clearly demonstrated as
such by tenfold documentary evidence. Has there
been any single spot in Italy, any instance of
republican agitation? Has there, during the last
two years, been formed a single line written privately
or publicly by us, or by the men representing the
principles of the party, pointing to a republic? Was
the question of the form of political institutions ever
mooted by us from the first beginnings of the
Italian movement?"

No! and let him who can, give me the lie, by
adducing facts to the contrary. Before the peace
of Villafranca, several among us protested against
entrusting our interests to foreign and despotic
armies; we knew from of old that no national
unity is formed in that way; they protested against

the sudden peace being made, and the dismembering
of Nice and Savoy.   After the peace of Villafranca,
when the emancipation of Italy became the work of
Italian arms, even those who had always abstained
from action hastened to join it without heeding
what banner dominated the movement.   The
monarchical programme of Garibaldi was adopted
by them.

On the 6th of October 1860 a Government Commissioner arrived in Naples from Palermo, bearer of
the Decree of Convocation of the Deputies of the
Sicilian people.   They had made Mordini fear an
intervention of Piedmontese troops at this juncture,
so that he desired to hurry on the day in which Sicily
should give its vote for union with the kingdom of
Italy.   A Sicilian Commission was spoken of, which
should go to Turin, and present itself to Cavour, with
the aim of asking protection against men to whom
anarchical principles were imputed, and who had imposed themselves on the country.   The news of an
assembly in the island annoyed Garibaldi.   The
danger of a similar occurrence twenty days before
had provoked the end of the Prodictatorship of
Depretis.   The General had several times declared
that when the war was ended a plebiscite should be
voted.   When we were informed that the Piedmontese had occupied the Marches and Umbria, he
spoke thus to his volunteers in his order of the day :
—"Our brothers are fighting the foreigner in the
very heart of Italy.   Let us go to meet them in
Rome to march with them thence to Venetian territory."   When he was asked to sanction the decree
of Mordini, and afterward to come to a deliberation
on the same subject with regard to Naples, he hesi-

tated to decide for an instant. After a few minutes of reflection, he said, with the manner of a man who rids himself of a great burden : "Since the state of things in Palermo cannot be changed without upsetting the Government again, order that another assembly should be called together at Naples."

On the 7th of October a council of ministers was held at the Palace, then the residence of the Marchese Pallavicini, who had been Prodictator for four days. The argument of annexation had often been discussed by the ministry with extreme warmth, especially on the first and second of the month, but without any result, the intentions of the General being known to all. On the seventh, encouraged by the example of the Sicilian Prodictatorship, and by Garibaldi's permission, the annexationists found a better way of expressing their intentions : it was decided by three votes against two that an assembly should be called together. I ignore whether from his own feeling or from counsels received from Turin, Pallavicini feared a congress of Neapolitan Deputies, he opposed it with all his power and left for Caserta, from whence he returned with orders from Garibaldi that in the mainland provinces they should vote by a plebiscite. And since the moment is opportune, and you, forgetting my labour and my pains, have only cast unmerited blame on things which deserved praise, allow me to make clear to those who ignore it, the part I took in these events and the opinions I held then. There are certain facts one does not discuss, but one feels. Can one discuss the existence of the sun, life, or humanity ? Discussion takes doubt for granted (or generates it ?), and is the cause of scepticism.

The nation exists as well as man, and it is not necessary that a people or a parliament should proclaim it so that it should exist.   Nevertheless, I could not make the unity of Italy, which has its basis in its geography, in its language, and in all those moral conditions that no one can ignore, depend on a yes or no, on the subtleties of rhetoricians, or the syllogisms of jurists.   But the lawful existence of Italy has been and is disputed, and its reconstruction has made the dynasties interested in its division our enemies, besides exciting the jealousies of the Great Powers.   The centuries had formed our poor fatherland piece by piece.   You may compare it to a polypus, which, being cut into pieces, and ignorant of being parts of a whole, lived each of them an autonomous and almost natural life.   So that in the ancient states, which disappeared with the Revolution, the Parliaments had come to discuss unity as a lawful form, and the federation we had all fought against might have arisen from this.   Chambers in general do not contain a great amount of good sense ; they generally represent history and traditions which sometimes fight against truth.   My own opinion was that the people should not establish national unity, nor constitute its forms, but declare their desire for it.   And then the assemblies, to whom the plebiscite should be law, would set about establishing the conditions of liberty and ability for it, so that the desire of the people should be actuated.   With this idea, and so that no injury should be done to the unity which was in the minds of all, and not yet an accomplished fact, I opposed the assembly in June 1860 in Palermo, and in the following September in Naples. The Decree of Mordini, unexpected as it was, and premature, upset our plans completely, because it was promulgated before the end of the war, and because it occasioned an assembly before the annexation. Obliged to defend it for the solidarity of the party, it was my desire and my care to find some way to guard against the dangers which threatened to ensue from it.

When Pallavicini announced to me that Garibaldi wished a plebiscite to take place, I saw immediately in this resolution the remedy to the ills I was fearing. Without disobeying Mordini, I thought one might conciliate his action with the will of the Dictator, and I immediately resolved to conduct things so that we should have a plebiscite first and an assembly after, and that the former should precede the latter.

The salvation of Italy seemed assured by this method.

On the 8th of October the ministers assembled in counsel in the room of the Presidency.

I stated the question; I reminded them of the engagements Garibaldi had taken with the country. I declared that the southern provinces, because of the special conditions of their revolution, because of their importance before the rest of Italy, could not accept the same form of plebiscite as Emilia and Tuscany. Our people should not give itself to another—not *annex* itself—(a verb which savours of dependence); it should *desire* the completion of unity. A plebiscite, according to the conditions of the central provinces, after Garibaldi had declared that we must go to Rome and drive the foreigner beyond the Alps, might be interpreted, not as a halt in our way, but as a renunciation of the complete redemption of the Peninsula. Italy had a powerful and seductive enemy in federation, so that we, in our plebiscite, ought to express an idea not unlike that which the convention proclaimed and applauded against the Federal doctrine of the Girondins—indicating to the people as a necessity of existence, and as their right, the unity and solidarity of the French Revolution. Pallavicini, who has the instinct of great and generous ideas, listened to me with attention, and exclaimed, " Well, we will decree Italy one and indivisible and Vittorio Emanuele her King. This is besides in conformity with the programme of Marsala."

The dominant idea of the plebiscite being agreed upon, various forms were considered, and that of Conforti was accepted. The decree was signed by all the ministers, and sent to the press. Naples should be proud of it. On that day a great principle was proclaimed and a solemn engagement taken, which we shall keep. You were then in that city, and you knew through the friends who surrounded me all that happened from the 6th of October onwards. I never had a counsel or a letter from you hostile to Monarchy. On the contrary, you sought to excuse yourself to those who feared in you a partisan of the Republic. Mario was at Garibaldi's side, and, according to your express wish, he remained ever near him till the 22nd of June. There is no doubt that your friend is more democratic even than yourself, since, ardent young man that he is, no one can reproach him in his political career of having offered his services to a prince. Mario, who was then devoted to you, could, if you had wished it, have done anything to combat the foundation of the Italian kingdom. Well, explain yourself; make your confession. What were your acts ? What were your words ? You said in a letter to me, which I have under my eyes, you were *like a man who hid himself, so as not to raise a cry of discord, and not to excite terror in public opinion*, that saw in your

name a challenge to the Principality.   You never proposed a programme different from that of Garibaldi.

The decree of the 8th of October founded the
basis of the new public rights in Italy.   Received
with enthusiasm by all assemblies, it gave a legal
consecration to the revolution that our arms were to
carry into the cities of the continent still occupied
by the foreigner.   For the first time three-eighths
of a great people were legislating in the interests of
all, of the free as of the fettered, discussing the
territorial sovereignty of the common fatherland,
and manifesting an express desire of conquering it ;
before that time only one cry had been heard from
the affranchised provinces, that of being united under
the constitution of Piedmont.   In the south this
method was not considered to be desirable, as it
seemed a surrender, but they claimed one right ; one
supreme duty was recorded for all the Latin race.
After this act it was necessary to proceed.   The
question of unity solved, it was necessary to prepare
ourselves to complete it, and to extend the decree
of the plebiscite to Sicily, and at the same time, the
scope of the assembly invoked in Palermo being
determined, another should be assembled in Naples.
On the night of the 8th I went to Caserta with the
Italian Envoy to explain ourselves to Garibaldi.   He
understood the utility of our project, and called
Pallavicini for the next day at 6 A.M.   What was
discussed between the General and his Prodictator
was unknown to me, since, being occupied in another
public service, I was not present at their interview.
Garibaldi told me the idea of an assembly had
been accepted ; so that when a fitting draft of a
decree was presented to him he approved it, and

wrote in his own hand the following words to
Pallavicini :—" All this seems to me what we agreed
upon with you, and is to my entire satisfaction.   If
you are of this opinion, send me a copy of the
present decree signed by you, and I will also sign
it."   Pallavicini misunderstood our idea ; I do not
know if he mistrusted me, because his friends in
Turin had described me unfavourably, or because he
thought me under your influence, whose opinions
he did not consider trustworthy.   What is certain is
that the Prodictator rejected the idea of an assembly
which he imagined could be changed into a constituent assembly, and would have led us on to a
Republic.   Scarcely had one spoken of it to him,
but, convinced of the dangers that he supposed would
ensue, he imputed to us the wish to cause a civil war.
The evening of the 11th October we met together at
Caserta around Garibaldi.   The discussion was violent,
and the result being favourable to my desires, Pallavicini
gave his resignation.   On the 12th all the ministers
followed his example, and the day passed in popular
demonstrations, in which *morte* and *viva* was cried
for all, and your name and mine were torn to tatters.
On the 13th a fresh council was held, to which
Pallavicini was called, also the ministers who had
retired, and a good number of the General's friends.
During the excitement of the speeches, while the
result of the discussion was uncertain, a petition of
the Neapolitan National Guard was received and a
letter from Ancona.   All were silent at a sign from
Garibaldi, who, after these documents were read,
gave his answer: " The plebiscite for Naples, and
the assembly for Sicily."   Leaving the room in
which this determination had been taken, without
the charge of a ministry, I received your draft of a

proclamation to the Neapolitans, which you asked
that the Dictator should sign, in which he insisted in
the convocation of the assembly. This paper arrived
late, but it is very important now to reveal to our
contemporaries what your ideas were then. I will
quote the principal periods, by which it will be seen
that you did not demand a rupture with the principality. You advised that Garibaldi should speak thus
to that population :—

"My programme, founded on the desire for the
greatest good of the Italian fatherland, cannot be
modified except as far as it shows itself contrary to
those sacred civil rights. The fear of cowards, or
party intrigues, cannot have any weight with me.

"Vittorio Emanuele being King of Italy, it is
necessary that Italy should exist; that Italy should
exist, it is necessary for her people to reconquer the
territory God gave her.

"He who denies the free action of this people,
and subordinates our emancipation to policy and to
the orders of a foreign government, is not, and
cannot be, favourable to our national unity; he does
not desire to see Vittorio Emanuele King of Italy in
Rome. I—and you, Neapolitans—do not belong to
that sad or deluded party."

The partisans of Count Cavour tried continually
to describe our intentions in false colours. We never
desired a constituent assembly, nor yet had we any
idea of working for a Republic. Our actions are a
guarantee of this, and a series of documents exist to
bear witness as to the projects which were not put
into action, which therefore never were published.
The evening of the 12th October 1850, when the
Prodictator and the ministers gave their resignation,

Garibaldi signed the decree by which an assembly of the representatives of the people was called together for the 11th of November in Naples. For this it was declared that the intention of the assembly should be to acknowledge the legality of all the procedure regarding the plebiscite, and to determine what would be necessary for the successive amalgamation of the southern provinces of the peninsula with Italy one and indivisible. Another decree of the same date, without changing the day of the reunion of the Sicilian assembly, explained its object, and called together the inhabitants of the island for the 28th October in their assemblies, so as to vote the plebiscite in the same manner as at Naples. These were the limitations with which the two assemblies were to work. That of Naples was opposed and repelled by exigencies which Garibaldi himself could not resist, and the Sicilian assembly was never convoked, owing to the alteration in Mordini's plans. The plebiscite of the southern states did not mean the annexation of the old Sicilian kingdom to the Sardinian provinces; if this had been implicitly understood it could not have been considered as immediate. The people declared their desire for national unity under the dynasty of Vittorio Emanuele. In this manner the constitutional principles of the future Government of our country were formed, and the honest men of the two contrary parties should have been satisfied, since by this course all possibility of either Federation or Republic was avoided. It was, however, necessary that the manner in which the unity was to be accomplished should be indicated by the assembly, since it could not be indicated by direct suffrage. Those who opposed themselves to this did not understand the

decree of the 8th of October, and betrayed its meaning. But they entrusted to the ministers at Turin
that which should have been the mission of local
parliaments.

Italy, by its physical constitution, never consisted
of a single state with uniform laws and constitutions,
in accordance with the conditions under which modern
states exist. Even under Roman sway the peninsula
had not an autonomous existence, but was an integral
part of that immense territory subjugated by the
right of the conquerors of the world; it was not
assimilated, but remained subdivided in its hundred
municipalities, which were each administered according to special laws. The work to which we had put
our hand, and which we were called to finish, was a
new one, and was to be done at a time in which
the axe of the conqueror was not permitted, because
there were no conquered people, and a radical change
was not ·possible, because the revolution was made in
the King's name. Many were the interests not to
be violently disturbed, and many rights had to be
respected. The transition of our provinces from
their state of isolation to that of association was
therefore very difficult, and a break in the gradual
progress of the populations towards unity bristled
with dangers.

There were two methods to compose the new
Italian family, and each of these was upheld by one of
the two schools aiming at governing the national
movement. The party having Cavour at its head,
and which had acted in concert with regular forces and
the artifices of diplomacy, held Piedmont as a banner
under which the several states of the Peninsula came
together. Our own, with Garibaldi at its head,
which had upset an ancient dynasty by the force of

its people's arms, considered Italy one and indivisible, the creation of a new state in which all monarchies were fused and disappeared, even including the Sardinian.   As a corollary to their premises, our adversaries regarded Piedmont as the principal body to which the other states were seeking annexation, and from which they were to receive laws and men to govern them.   They did not understand the vices of this system and the dire consequences which would ensue from it, and the dangers to unity.   It was the same as to drive and enclose in a narrow circle, in which was already four million and a half of people, seventeen million more, which war and revolution had liberated from despotism.   Either all would have been asphyxiated, or the last comers, crippled in a place incapable of holding so many people, would have broken the boundary, rebelling against the ancient inhabitants who, being at home, naturally considered themselves masters.

We proposed a quite different state of things for the organisation of Italy.   In the peninsula there should be neither first nor last.   From 1848 to 1860 every one had done his part in the emancipation of the nation.   In the new partnership the provinces should bring each one its patrimony of experience and doctrine, and all should participate equally in the benefits proceeding from a new order of things, and consequently share the necessary burden of maintaining it.

In Italy at the time there was no model state whose laws and hegemony could be adopted without examination.   Piedmont, which had saved the national standard in the shipwreck of Italian liberty, had dragged along till 1860 with many codes of despotic government, and has not purged itself from several yet, notwithstanding the constitution of the kingdom of Italy. The southern provinces, on the contrary, however much they might be wanting in political guarantees, in extreme contrast to the tyranny which repressed independent thought, were before all in civil progress by the excellence both of code and administration ; so that with a few changes which liberty had fostered, the State could be used as the basis of the nation's legislation.

This, from the moment of our first entrance into Naples, had been the intention of the Dictatorship. The kingdom which, after the annexation of Tuscany and Emilia, had formed itself in the west of the Peninsula was, by the importance of its population, inferior to the country over which Garibaldi ruled. The new laws proclaimed towards the end of 1859 had not been tried in Piedmont ; they had caused irritation in all Lombardy, and had not been accepted in Florence. If the southern provinces had reformed the administration and the codes, to suit the new political institutions, and had satisfied the interests of the multitude with good economic laws, they would have satisfied the interests of the multitude, and we should have arrived at unity without the losses which later on the emissaries sent from Turin brought about, and we should have brought the rest of the nation to that progress which is still to come.

It was forbidden to the Dictatorship to work out these reforms. In the course of one day we had decreed the abolition of the lottery, the suppression of the monasteries, and the confiscation of the church property. The law on monasteries was withdrawn before it was officially published ; the working out of the other two reforms was postponed. The beneficent will of Garibaldi being paralysed by a bad genius who combated his counsels, it was better, and would have been more in accordance with civil prudence, to depute the work of regeneration, to which the head of the State should aspire, to the popular assembly.

The Annexationists hastened to put a rein on the populations of the south. But concerning this I have less to say, but more of the method we ourselves followed as promoters of the revolution. This method is entirely your own, and to you therefore must be imputed, as its author, as well as to ourselves who accepted it, all the consequences which logically ensued from it. You certainly did not unwillingly conceive the formation of the Italian kingdom as an enlargement of that of Savoy. That after the plebiscite of the 21st of October it had fused into a new state did not enter into your mind. To prove it I have but to read the petitions you drew up on the 20th of November 1860 for the removal of the French from Rome. Not only you bent before the throne, but you adopted the process of annexation according to Cavour. In the petition to the King of Italy you wrote : "Sire, Italy is being born again. Its nationality is now an accomplished fact. We were only yesterday four million and a half of Sardinian subjects ; we are to-day twenty-two millions of Italians, bound together in concord around one common banner."

Nor is it to be wondered at. Piedmont becoming Italy ; these Sardinian subjects multiplying and changing name, from the first day that Carlo Alberto assumed the crown, was for you the beginning from which the development of national unity took place.

On this argument you might at the time have enunciated different theories in writing, but in practice you always acted as though unity could only be accomplished through the King's power, and that the people over which he reigned by strength of treaties was the nucleus around which the other populations of the Peninsula would gather. From 1831 to 1860 your looks were always turned towards Piedmont. By inviting the Prince of that State to command the battles of the fatherland, you designated him, even against your will, to the people as the future head of the nation. When a king is invited to take part in any undertaking and accepts, it is Utopian to presume that he comes an equal among equals; he always will be—though chosen and not imposed—a leader and commander. Naturally, in this partnership of monarchy and democracy you find more exposed to sacrifices but farther from honours and influence, the patriots who distinguished themselves most in conspiracy and at the barricades, the new Power feeling some diffidence towards those who became destroyers of other crowns. It resulted from this that the individuals whom nature furnished with servile souls, and who through mere chance or the inexperience of the combatants gave authority in the first ranks of the revolution, found it easy to get rid of independent men, and were not wanting in means to prevent the people from manifesting their desires and providing for their needs. A new throne excites false hopes because all the ambitious flock round it, and new courtesans, so as to be welcomed and not to be turned away, surround it with suspicions and keep independent citizens in the distance. Your insurrectional strategy also was at fault. When in 1850 you constituted the National

Committee, it was not possible to convince you that the basis of our movements should be in the south. You threw all the funds of the loan into Lombardy and Emilia, with the intention of inciting a revolutionary movement in the north and in the centre of our country. I will not remind you of the plots as early as 1852, in which Tito Speri, the priest Grisli, and other friends worthy of a better lot, fell victims ; it will suffice that I should speak of those which followed.

In 1853 the campaign was opened in Milan by the audacious daggers of 6th February. In September the expedition of Sarzana followed and the preparations of bands of men on the mountains of Cadore. In 1854 you changed provinces, but not country ; in May you ordered a descent of armed men in Lunigiana, and towards August in Lomellina ; then you prepared movements in Como, and again at Milan, which would have been in insurrection if the Austrian police had not been more quick than you, or than that fearless phalanx of martyrs who left their lives in the hands of the executioner. If in Lombardy and Emilia your work had been crowned with success, Piedmont would have joined and have consequently planted her banner there. A monarchy cannot permit an insurrection to triumph on her frontiers. It is a necessity of its existence, if it does not quell a popular rising, at least to dominate it by turning it to its own advantage. It is like a fire at a neighbouring house, which it would be foolish to permit to extend, because one would run the risk of being involved and suffocated by it.

This was not foreign to the logic of your conspiracies. Through conspiring, it was your intention to force the King into a war with Austria. You were not only convinced that in case of victory beyond the Ticino the field would not remain in the possession of the citizens, but you thought that after the five days had passed, the regular troops would have come to the rescue, would have laid siege to the fortresses and have cleared the ground of foreign forces. To you the volunteers on the barricades could only be the forerunners of the Piedmontese army. This idea dominated the expedition of the intrepid Pisacane also. In that bold but much-to-be-deplored episode of the Italian Revolution you decided on Genoa as the point of departure of the war which should have ensued. In 1857, while planning the movement of Sapri, you did not intend to bring forward in your native Liguria a Republican Government. Your adversaries accused you of this, but you denied. Your idea was to occupy the Arsenal and surprise the King's fleet, in order to direct it against Naples. If this plan had prospered and its details had been followed out, a conflict between the two dynasties which then reigned at the two extremities of the Peninsula would have been inevitable. Even in this case, unity would have come through monarchy.

In order that the revolution should develop itself independently and free from Piedmontese influence it should have broken out through the indigenous forces of the south of the Peninsula. Between the southern kingdom and the Sardinian were the central provinces, so that there would have been no necessity for the House of Savoy to intervene, nor would its interference have been tolerated, and the tyrant would have been alone with his subjects in this duel in which they had engaged themselves.

Naples and Sicily were in continual agitation. After the events of 1848 and the fierce reaction following, it was not possible for the country to absolve the Bourbons. Setting hatred aside, the innocent blood which flowed on the 15th of May, and the brutal burning of great cities, would have incited the people, by their own instinct and in homage to tradition, to have reasserted their liberty.

The people of the south are extremely practical. Educated from an early date to monarchical institutions which were tempered by the autonomy of municipalities or by the authority of assemblies, one may say that absolute government was for them of recent origin, and was of short duration.

In eight and a half centuries of the southern kingdom no prince (all were, be it remarked, foreigners) took root in that country. Of the nine dynasties that succeeded them four died out between the walls of the palace itself, and of the others some were expelled, and those who remained until the usurpation was established never lived in quiet.

The Bourbons tried to debase and humiliate the people, but the native character prevailed over the infernal acts of the Court. Science, with Bruno and Campanilla, with Giannone and Pagano, always rebelled against despotism, and in time the people arose more powerful than its despots.

Sicily had not forgotten the vespers, nor Naples the struggles against Charles V., and contemporaries remembered the miracles of courage and of civic strength of 1799 and of 1848. . . .

As early as February 1850 some Calabrian friends and I remembered the necessity of endeavouring to get up an insurrectional movement in our native provinces in order to begin the revolution in the south. I insisted on this in December, suggesting that the weight of the yoke in the island was such that the citizens would have followed any course offering them the initiative of enfranchisement. You answered the 27th of the same month :—" You are right in your manner of seeing things in Sicily ; the people must be so weary that they would be ready to embrace any course of action suggested to them. For this reason it is necessary for us to work, and that the initiative should start from us ; and if we accomplish the loan it will start."

The loan was made, but the initiative was neither from Sicily nor Naples. There was worse. Seeing the forces of the party consumed in bold but in-efficacious attempts in 1853, I again wrote to you in the same strain, and your answer on the 23rd of December was :—" As to the commencement, I am passive."

You thought of the southern provinces in 1857 after the war in the Crimea, and in 1859 after the descent of the French into Italy. At that time a rival interest to ours prevailed over the people. The time after 1854 had passed to our prejudice, for the National Committee, which was upheld by the prestige, and under the shadow, of Count Cavour, was disputing our ground.

You will remember how we worked so that Sicily should be in insurrection the 4th of October 1859. All was ready, when a letter from Turin sufficed to arrest the action of the conspirators. Many of those who conspired with us were in correspondence with La Farina. In my journey through the island I had found in the same hands and on the same table the

Piccolo Corriere, a publication of the moderate party, and your own paper, *Pensiero ed Azione*.

In order to conciliate the two parties then militant, and to strengthen the revolution, not by my initiative, but by your own desire, we were on the 10th of December 1859 in negotiation with the Dictator of Emilia. A few days later Rosalino turned to Garibaldi and had a promise of help from him.

After these alliances any question as to the form of government would have been inopportune. Garibaldi, holding out his hand to us, would not have altered his programme, and Farini would have denied us all subsidies for proclaiming a Republic at Palermo.

Long was the way we were obliged to go over, but it was not achieved without advantage. And at the point we have arrived at it is time to ask, Who was the author of this situation ?

To this question you shall answer yourself :— " History will remember that *we*, honouring the judgment of the people for love of Garibaldi, through the desire to try any means towards concord, threw at the feet of Monarchy our ideas, our hopes, our presentiments, our memories, and our power of agitating, also the favour for Italy in the eyes of Europe which we had obtained, our influence on the working classes and thousands of young men educated by our doctrines. It will be remembered that after Villafranca all of us—people, volunteers, writers —took part in the interrupted work. We instigated the annexations of the central provinces; we instigated the Sicilian insurrection, the Neapolitan uprising ; we accepted, although outraged and culumniated, the monarchical programme of Garibaldi ; we applauded the plebiscite, which gave to Monarchy ten millions

of free men . . . freed by their own arms and that of
Garibaldi." You wrote this in an address to the
Italians in September 1862.

The kingdom of Italy is your work, our work,
and that of the men who, being in the adversaries'
camp, took part in the revolution. Up to this time
it is incomplete, but you may be sure it will be completed. If sense and daring do not fail, it will not
be long before we have the entire enclosure of the
Alps and the two seas with Rome for its capital.

In any case, would it be a plausible motive that,
not having been able to complete the national edifice,
for which in other countries centuries have laboured,
we should throw it down in order to rebuild it on
new foundations?

Would this be the wise act of serious men?

Putting our hand to the hammer, should we not be
running the risk of repeating the labour of Sisyphus?

I know; I have never forgotten it, and have
repeated it frequently in the Chamber, that you are
the precursor of unity. The idea of the nation
Dante set forth in his immortal writings became an
apostleship to you. Nevertheless, I know also that
you held complete unity above all forms, and that to
it you sacrificed several times the triumph of democracy. Now I should not consent, and with all my
strength I will oppose, that the conquest the nation
has made for its unity should be sacrificed in order
that the democratic principle should prevail.

Before 1860 I understood an insurrection in the
name of a different principle from that which Italy
accepted later, because at that time, although the
question was complicated by the war in Lombardy
and by the occurrences in Emilia, a choice was still
possible. Afterwards the force of events was too

great for us, and their logic showed us the path we had to follow.

It remains a fact which we cannot dispute that, after thirty years of struggle and martyrdom, neither party had power to effect national unity. The monarchical party in 1859 stopped at Cattolica, and we, in 1860, revolting in the south, had to go to meet them in order to constitute this kingdom of twenty-two million of citizens. If the union of these two forces led us to such useful results, combined action will do the rest.

You do not believe it, and because I do, you impute to me the desire to pay homage to power, and infer that were I to see you the more powerful to-morrow I would again return to you.

You ought to have remembered above all that I have never been a coward. In the brief course of years when I was conspiring with you I admired your genius, I respected your faith, but I did not perceive any strength in you. I faced many dangers at your behest, but while risking my life I was not foolish enough to hope that if I fell into the hands of the enemy you would have come to save my head from the executioner's axe.

I respect you as a man. If you were in power, if you were named triumvir, I would have nothing more to do with you.

For the tendencies to Guicciardini's teachings which you pretended to discover in me I might return the compliment. Since 1831 you have not been faithful to the Republic. Could you explain to me why from time to time deserting it you approached Monarchy?

No, friend! in our country no one is strong; only Italy can be so where her sons are united in the love of country and have the conscience of their duties. And that Italy should be strong, and that her strength should not be dissolved, I defend the work of the plebiscite.

After the event of 1860 our method and circumstances in the Italian movement changed entirely. Parties and insurrections inside the frontiers of the new kingdom became an anachronism ; and for us who had claimed unity with monarchy, they would have amounted to crime. Having accepted a system and called on the multitude to accept it, one cannot conspire against it without being wanting in logic and loyalty.

It would not have been logical after having decreed the plebscite of the 21st of October, to hasten to tear it up.

It would not have been loyal after having invited the people to vote for Vittorio Emanuele, to promote the making of a republic.

One loses the credit to which every honest man should aspire, and scepticism takes possession of people's souls when from day to day opposite judgments are enounced on the same institution.

Political change kills a party, which owes it to itself to behave coherently if it does not wish to succumb under the weight of its own contradictions.

I do not deny my past, and I pride myself on my old beliefs.

After the heroic defences of Rome and Venice, the Republic was my ideal, and I was convinced that it could alone constitute the nation.

It may have been the effect of the education of the people, which certainly was not our work ; perhaps it was due to the skill of our adversaries, who

knew how to be beforehand and to appear more united;
perhaps to the influence of Garibaldi's name, who,
proclaiming unity in the kingdom, divided the
militant democracy in two parts, that our previsions
failed and we were the first who had to accept the
national programme, " Italy and Vittorio Emanuele."

Conquered by circumstances, on the 18th of
February 1861 I entered Parliament and remained
faithful to my new engagements, my hand on my
heart and my eyes on Italy, my guiding star through
all my life.

A soldier of national right, I was always ready to
step into the breach to defend the rights of the
people, its guarantees and its liberty.

My successes at the urn were rare during the five
years of the new kingdom, but my triumphs over
hearts were not rare.

Besides, one must credit a deputy not only with
the good he has done, but also for the ills which
he has known how to avoid. . . .

I have never understood the theory of parliamentary resignation. The soldier even when wounded,
as long as his arm is vigorous enough to hold his
gun, holds it his duty not to abandon the field to
the enemy; when he retires, his act may not be
considered as the result of cowardice, but will always
be the consequences of blameworthy despair. . . .

To me an oath is a serious matter, and I admired
Alberto Mario, who refused to be deputy rather than
take it.

If the Republicans in Italy had wished to remain
true to their faith, they ought to have kept themselves out of the military and political movements
of 1859, and later, and waited to begin action when
the trial of Monarchy should fail.

It is unworthy of a gentleman to enter into the
Temple of Legislature, to take an oath to respect it,
and to seize an opportune moment to come out of
it, his soul soiled with perjury.

If I had to serve the country under such
conditions I should refuse, preferring to retire an
unknown citizen between the walls of private life.
I have given up my whole being to Italy, to its
well-being, and sacrificed the political principles that
I had cultivated since my earliest years ; I will not,
I must not sacrifice on its altar the purity of my
conscience.   This is the only possession remaining to
me after having spent in exile and in revolutions the
small patrimony of my forefathers.

You ask if my conscience has fixed any limit to
Monarchy, and if the men who esteemed me and
loved me as a brother will meet me on their path
again, a brother through the course of events.

The question proves to me that you and I are
at the antipodes in the matter of juridical theories.

Before all one has to ascertain what you mean by
Monarchy.   The King, or the institution which he
is at the head of?

Is it the King?

By the fundamental laws of the country he is
outside all political questions ; quite neutral in the
struggle of opinions.   From this state of things,
comes the English aphorism which you ought to
know better than I.   *The King can do no ill.*

While living in London, I heard Prince Albert
blamed for certain decisions of the Crown ; he was
a member of the Privy Council and took part in
all Cabinet affairs, but I never heard that any news-
paper or individual held the gracious Queen respon-

sible for the errors of Palmerston or Derby, of Gladstone or Disraeli.

Is it the institution of which the King is at the head ?

Is it worth what it is desired to be by the men of whom it consists ; by the Parliament and the Ministers ?

It depends on them to interpret and put into practice the laws to restrain or extend the use of liberty, to limit or develop political guarantees, to offend or respect the rights of the citizen, to raise up or humiliate the dignity of the nation.

We have now in many provinces of the south the military *régime*, and they have had (I repeat your words) :

The state of siege.

The imprisonment of certain deputies.

The dissolution of democratic associations.

The frequent prohibition of public meetings.

The prosecution of the press.

The violation of personal liberty.

The refusal to the Venetians and to the Romans of the rights of citizenship in the kingdom.

We have had Turin stained with blood.

These events are deplorable, and I did not fail to blame the authors of such a state of things. The ministers who ordered them, and the Chamber that tolerated them, can never be absolved by history. Nevertheless, could you tell me in good faith that monarchy is responsible for such acts?

Let us turn over the page ; we shall read that even worse things happened under a popular government beyond the Alps.

In 1848 the Republic was proclaimed in Paris, and a few months after the French had—

The state of siege.

The capital was bombarded.

The representatives of the people were persecuted and obliged to go into exile to avoid being imprisoned.

The liberty of the press was suspended.

Independent journalists were arrested.

Popular assemblies were closed.

Public meetings were prohibited.

They fired on the people *en masse*.

There were deportations without trial to Nukaiva.

These violent deeds against the most civilised people in Europe would hardly be attributed by you to the Republic!

Constitutional monarchies or republics, if the men who are at their head become the prey of terror, are changed into tyrannical government. For this reason I maintain that the good or the ill of any institution depends on those who make it.

In Italy the errors and mistakes of these latter years must be imputed to party spirit.

The men who in 1860 hastened to wrest power from our hands did not know how to make use of the elements of order which existed in ancient kingdoms; they destroyed everything and made every one discontented without having the power of giving stability to the new kingdom. So much so, that the Peninsula has all its means and its resources still intact to receive the power of a great state. The man only is wanting, and he will not fail to appear who, raising it up and giving it fresh life, shall give health and vigour to the generous invalid.

A people in the exercise of its rights has as much

T

liberty as is the total of political guarantees conceded by law.

These guarantees are extended by time and are broken up by fear; they last generally more through the prudence of the people than through the uprightness of magistrates.

I have never said that the constitution of the 4th of March is a model *of perfection*. It is not even the best of those published in 1848.

If there should exist fundamental laws that can be said to constitute the *Ark of liberty*, containing every germ of future progress, it would be those deliberated on the 10th of July 1848 by the Sicilian Parliament. A deputy in the House of Commons that voted the fall of the Bourbons, my judgment cannot come under suspicion as to a monarchical constitution, whose ideas and style were imitated from the French charter of 1830.

The kingdom of Italy has a constitution which, whatever it may be, is the basis of a political system which we have to improve. The change, instead of coming about through barricading the streets and fighting among ourselves, I propose should be accomplished by enlightening the minds of the people, and making those principles triumphant at the electoral urn which we desire should prevail in the laws of the State. You say no! and preach insurrection. I say yes! and preach the liberty of discussion at the tribune, in the press, and in public meetings.

You declare that such a system can only exist in England and in no other states, which, according to you, would seem to be condemned to consume themselves by oscillating between despotism and revolution.

Since 1789 every form of political government

has been tried in Europe, and none has endured. Let us inquire into the cause of this instability, and let us at the same time return to the beginning of the British Government so as to learn the causes which allowed it to take root in a country which was also wet with the blood of its martyrs.

That a government should have a solid basis, it is necessary that it should be the consequence of a gradual and progressive evolution of the past. If it should be a foreign importation, or if it should arise by violating the habits of the people and without respecting the national traditions, the country is launched on an adventurous future, and is obliged to endure new upheavings and to try fresh experiments.

I shall besides remark that in order that reforms should be acceptable, and that they should enter into the government of the country, they should not attack the private or common interests of the country suddenly, before having created fresh ones which would take the place of the old.

Man fights readily for his interest, and not always for what he considers to be his right. So that a legislator accomplishes his mission ill who, forgetting the interests of the individual or those of the multitude, gives a rational government to the nation at one cast, which might be admirable as a work of art, but would be too platonic to succeed when put into practice.

France in 1791 did not modify itself, but broke with history, and what were the consequences? In sixty years it has nine times changed its government and its constitution, it has proclaimed and destroyed two republics, and finds itself to-day (1865) where it was at the beginning of the century.

The other foreign continental powers followed its example and suffered the same crisis. An insurrection in Paris, when not preceded, was always followed by insurrections in Italy. We went to seek from this civilised but excitable city not only its fashions but its constitution and its laws. As these did not suit our habits, and did not agree with the ideas we accepted, they fell as easily as they had been adopted.

The method in which Great Britain progressed was very different. The constitution of 1215, inferior in political guarantees to that which the Sicilians had given themselves in 1296 and held till 1815, had been during six centuries and a half so enlarged and altered, that in comparing it now and then one can scarcely recognise its origin. Nevertheless, it is not yet a finished work, and in some respects is inferior to the Italian constitution of the 4th of March.

The English constitution grew with the nation. As the country progressed towards unity, public right made further advances.

This historical process is notably observable in one of the most important liberties the British people enjoys—that of conscience and worship.

With the Tudors the laws of intolerance against those not belonging to the Anglican Church scarcely found any equal in the decrees of the Holy Inquisition. At the death of Elizabeth, when England and Scotland became united under one prince, the spirit of religious independence so much agitated society that it combined to obtain the *Toleration Bill*, which abolished every punishment for Protestants who were outside the official religion.

In 1800 the Irish Parliament was suppressed.

That of Scotland having also been abolished in 1707, the political unity of the kingdom was accomplished, and a few years later, as a consequence, the law of the emancipation of Catholics was established.

These reforms, as you know, did not come about all at once, faith in the working of time being the great strength of the English.

The law of tolerance was passed eighty-six years after the death of Elizabeth, and the one in favour of Catholics twenty-nine years after the law of union. Even after this one cannot say that liberty of conscience and of worship was established by law, although it was by custom. Up to the year 1858 the Jews could not sit in Parliament, and even now being a Catholic priest is a reason for ineligibility.

I could, by pursuing my examination, remind you of how the English constitution became altered in other respects. The regal power, now limited, was more extended under the Plantagenets; it was immoral under the Tudors, violent at the time of the Stuarts, intriguing with George III.; and the legislative power, in which after 1832 the House of Commons held the control, had been before ruled by the all-powerful will of the Peers. I must further mention the suspicious laws against meetings, not abrogated, but fallen into disuse, and discuss the manner in which personal liberty and inviolability of the dwelling was consolidated.

The English have had the good sense never to destroy but to modify their institutions. They have held firmly to the continuity of natural right. In 1641 and in 1688 they established fresh warrants of public liberty, but they never thought of writing a new constitution. The Republic being proclaimed, they changed nothing in the political organisation except the king, for whom the Protector was substituted. Parliament continued to work as usual.

Now I will ask you, I will ask all Italians, why should we not follow the example of the English? Must we then necessarily, imitating French example, continue in the vicious circle of insurrections and revolutions?

You will tell me that in Great Britain the aristocracy is a basis to the system, and that the traditions of several centuries are sufficient to consolidate the political rule we so much admire.

Certainly these are not reasons which should discourage us. The aristocracy in that country is only territorial, and in the great economic movement going on daily, it feels itself having no part in the financial and industrial element. The true foundation of English society is the House of Commons, to which is added a spirit of independence and individual action, that autonomy of man which in many cases does not make the intervention of the Government necessary and makes a nation powerful.

Macaulay tells that the Tories, who represented authority and tradition, and the Whigs, who were protectors of progress, twice in the interests of their country, torn by anarchy, felt the necessity to suspend discussion and to unite their forces in a common aim. Their first coalition was at the death of Cromwell, and served to restore Monarchy ; the second coalition was in 1688, when James II. was dethroned and the Bill of Rights decreed ; they then called William of Orange to the throne of Great Britain.

The era of revolution was then closed, and the

tradition of an orderly and progressive constitutional *régime* began.

It is time that Italy should have the same strength if it desires the completion of unity.

To do this, it is necessary that the redemption of the fettered provinces should be accomplished by this kingdom of twenty-two millions of citizens, and that the statute of the 4th of March should be the point of departure to political progress.

One cannot avoid this alternative. Every other method would be fallacious; every other way would lead as to a precipice.

As you see, I have entirely opened my heart to you; my intentions in the past, my fears and my hopes in the future, are no longer secret.

I ignore what you would say, and I also ignore what your new friends would say, for I fear they have not all the same merit as your old friends, some of them resembling you with the likeness an ape has to a man.

The kingdom of Italy is an accomplished fact to which you were not alien, although you may have repented having helped in its formation.

I am now, what I was before entering Parliament; what Rosalino Pilo was the 27th of March 1860, when leaving for Sicily, an obstinate partisan of unity. If there has been in me a change as to the method of the national work, it dates from then, and you cannot impute it to me as a crime, as no one will accuse you of one, since we have preserved the unity which is the life of Italy, as a sovereign condition, the supreme form above all others.

Until December 1859 I put all my energies into

a revolution of the south with the local forces, independently of any influence of the adverse party.

When the alliance with Garibaldi was made and his programme accepted, I delayed the hour of the plebiscites, believing it necessary to the success of the national cause that they should be voted when the war was over.

When delays were no longer possible, I repelled the formula for the annexation of Naples and Sicily to Piedmont, and I had the unity and indivisibility of our fatherland proclaimed, an unchangeable pledge which no one can break without getting out of the compact, making every action violating it null and void.

The plebiscites once decreed, it remained to the assemblies to recognise the work relating to them, and to prepare the southern provinces of the Peninsula for their incorporation to United Italy.   My attempts were not always successful.

On the 21st of October 1860 a legal act was drawn up, against which I cannot rebel, since it incorporates the expression of the national will.   You, after having recognised it till September 1862, oppose it, and desire your friends to do likewise.   In this I can never be of your opinion, and I find that Garibaldi is not either, for he remains true to the banner that he unfurled, glorious and uncontaminated, in 1859 and in 1860.

I feel the obligation to remain on the ground I have reached through your and my own actions and the irresistible logic of events.   It is a basis to future operations ; it is the *ubi sistam* of Archimedes, acquired by so much trouble and so many dangers, and which cannot be abandoned without running into fresh disasters.

The political government of the kingdom is a thousand miles from being perfect. But it is of no use harrying it with divisions, inciting the people to them, or to the barricades. It is our duty to correct it, to reform it, to build it up, as the English have done and are doing, by the means of their charters. It is prudent to recognise in our proceedings the limitations of human progress, and not precipitate ourselves forward to attain it, as our haste would make us lose what we have gained. During the five years of the new kingdom it might have done more and better work, but lost time is not regained by impatience or despair. Restore calm to your troubled soul ; trust in the strength of the country ; enlighten the people without exciting it.

INDEX

Numbers after 224 refer to Appendix

THE END

www.ingramcontent.com/pod-product-compliance
Lightning Source LLC
Chambersburg PA
CBHW020855020726
47497CB00005B/1423